...his stance wi
seemingly bolted t
surveyed every de   ⌄. ⅏⅏⅏ environment with the
presence of someone whose self-confidence couldn't
easily be shaken. He carried himself like he belonged
here. Hell, like he owned the place. The startling
combination of blue eyes, the color of glacier water,
against an olive complexion and full black beard
created a commanding presence. Glued like a sentry
next to the man, Wager, the farm's border collie exuded
absolute devotion with his tongue lolling out and head
tilted up to the hand stroking him.

*Jesus, who IS that dude? He can't be a new buyer
interested in our foals the way Wager is fawning all
over him but he's someone important, no doubt. Focus,
Ariel, you're here to work, not get infatuated with the
first cowboy who comes along.*

As if he sensed her curiosity, the enigmatic
stranger turned his attention toward her. The intensity
of his stare invaded her comfort zone as he coolly and
completely assessed her with a visual review of her
body that left her feeling undressed. The hair on her
arms stood erect. She rubbed them as if removing a
chill. The physical reaction was her own intuitive
warning system and experience had taught her to listen
to her body. She understood all too well about arrogant,
possessive men. Her controlling ex-boyfriend was a
moral zero and the most deceptive man she'd ever met.
The image of him sent shivers skidding down her spine
but she quickly thrust the memories aside. *He's out of
my life and nowhere near here.*

Ariel slid the dog tags back and forth on the chain
she wore around her neck...

Forever in Ocala

by

Connie Y Harris

The Forever Series

Forever in Ocala

Cover Art by *Kim Mendoza*

The Wild Rose Press, Inc.
PO Box 708
Adams Basin, NY 14410-0708
Visit us at www.thewildrosepress.com

Publishing History
First Champagne Rose Edition, 2016
Print ISBN 978-1-5092-0643-8
Digital ISBN 978-1-5092-0644-5

The Forever Series
Published in the United States of America

Dedication

To my daughter, Dr. Ariel Womble,
a healer and a wise old soul.
This book is dedicated to you and all the women like
you who chose equine medicine as your profession.
Thank you for nurturing the magnificent beast
we love so much.

Acknowledgments

Special thanks to Don Tinnin, Navy SEAL and a fine sailor to boot, who served as my technical adviser and ensured I colored between the lines in portraying these brave warriors.

~*~

To Lynette and Melissa, the critiquing queens, for insisting I write it better.

~*~

To my editor, my mentor and my confidante, Donna Confer, there aren't enough superlatives.

Chapter 1

Somewhere in Kumar Province, Afghanistan

The deadly blast hurled Gavin Cross off the Humvee and propelled him head first onto the rocky Afghan roadside. Deafened by the explosion and blinded from the debris raining down on him, the battle-hardened SEAL struggled to regain his situational awareness. He sucked spittle into his mouth and spat out a clump of sand. "What the fuck?"

His temples throbbed in pain so intense he saw double. Gavin shook his head and blinked until his vision cleared and the deafening buzz ringing in his ears lessened. He located his rifle a few feet away and snaked forward on his elbows, ignoring the pain-induced urge to vomit. With his weapon retrieved, he rolled toward a prominent boulder for cover. Peering around the edge of the rock he located what remained of the Humvee. The explosion had flipped the vehicle upside down and one of the men he was assigned to protect groaned in agony, as he lay pinned beneath its hulking metal frame. *He needs a corpsman. Got to get him out of here.* A second figure sprawled lifeless across the detached steering wheel half-buried in the nearby embankment.

Gavin cursed and ducked at the familiar pinging sound of metal striking metal. *A sniper.* The second bullet zipped over his head and ricocheted off the Humvee, kicking up a cloud of dust close to the trapped soldier. Too close. The recent round was meant for the young Marine Lieutenant trapped under the Humvee. Fortunately, the Taliban dude was a bad shot.

The high ground above the road was a perfect hiding place for the enemy so Gavin scanned along the ridge for the next flash of sunlight reflecting off the steel frame of an AK47. "There's the tango," he muttered as an earth-toned turban popped up and took aim at the Humvee below. Gavin raised his weapon, cleared his mind of the ambient noise and slowed his breathing. The rifle's scope provided a perfect visual of the target as he positioned the man's head in the front sight. Surrounded in a cocoon of calm concentration, his index finger coiled around the trigger. He squeezed.

"Take that, you son of a bitch," he growled, confirming his hit as a cloud of bloody red mist sprayed and the sniper's body crumpled behind the crest of the ridge.

****

Bagram Air Base, Afghanistan

Gavin directed his gaze to the dark night as the distant sky lit up, spreading a phosphorous glow over the horizon. Heavy mortar fire rained down on an unseen enemy hiding in the mountainous terrain.

Somewhere in the distant hills the terrorists were getting hammered. *Better the tangos than us.*

"Hey Cross, having another sleepless night?" Tony Franco, Gavin's teammate, called out as he rounded the corner of the barracks.

"Yeah man. Heavy artillery is not my favorite lullaby. What about you?" Gavin tapped the crystal of his wristwatch. "Almost two A.M. and you barreled around the corner like your ass was on fire."

The Petty Officer and Gavin's closet friend, joked, "Dude, you know the life of a corpsman on the Teams. I'm always patching up some asshole who stepped out in front of a bullet."

Gavin laughed. "C'mon T-man, isn't stitching up our bullet holes better than treating those low life gang bangers at UCLA's emergency room? You know," he chuckled as he positioned his hands in the form of scale, "gunshot versus stab wound. Besides, there is no finer bunch of hard-asses to hang with than SEAL Team 2. Right?"

"Roger that, Caveman," Tony grinned, switching to Gavin's nickname. All the team guys had alternate names, specifically designed to nag and elicit a response. Unmerciful teasing was part of the SEAL culture. An appropriate nickname, which sparked repeated volleys of sarcastic banter sufficed. The handle was usually assigned right after some supremely stupid escapade in which alcohol had a major involvement. But all the ribbing and joking served a purpose and was a part of life in this elite brotherhood. The camaraderie built an impenetrable unit. These were men who always had each other's back, no matter what.

Tony looked skyward as the whump, whump, whump of low flying helicopters grew louder and invaded the surrounding air space sending clouds of desert sand swirling around the men. Pebbles from the dry dust pinged against their helmets and protective eye gear.

"Delta fire team's approaching," Tony yelled, as he looked left to locate Gavin. "Incoming, wounded on board. Time to hustle, bro."

"I'm right behind you, Franco." Gavin cupped his hands around his mouth amplifying his voice over the racket and noticed they were shaking. Sweat trickled from his hairline and pooled above the rubber lip of his plastic glasses. He quickly swiped the salty drops off with his shirt-covered forearm. *Shake off the bullshit, Cross.* He wiped the sweat away, but couldn't stop his hands from shaking.

His arms se-sawed back and forth in a faked, casual motion as he jogged up to Tony.

"You okay, Cross?" The corpsman's brows creased as he spoke.

"Yeah, why?"

"You're shaking." Tony leaned in closer, "and your pupils are dilated." He grabbed Gavin's wrist, checking his heart rate. "Your pulse is racing."

"What are you, my fucking mother?" Gavin yanked his arm away. "Let's get the wounded off the bird and set up triage. You can be my mommy later." He tamped down the anger and threw a 'what the hell,' smile back to Tony. *Damn it.* What was happening to him? He'd seen other men fall apart on the battlefield and swore he'd never allow this shit to get into his head.. The men on his team needed a strong leader and he was their man. He couldn't afford to let any weakness show. If he could only get a good night's sleep; one without nightmares and waking up in sweat-drenched sheets with stink so strong it clogged his nostrils, he'd be okay.

****

"Hey Chief," Tony rapped on the door and parked himself in the doorway for the chief to acknowledge him, not sure if he really wanted to have this conversation.

Chief O'Malley looked up from his computer screen. "Come on in Franco. Shut the door and take a seat. I got a report we unloaded some wounded off the last operation, but no casualties, right?"

Tony closed the door and shifted to the closest chair, "Yeah, a few shrapnel cuts and minor bullet wounds but nothing life threatening." He frowned. "Chief, I'd like a word with you about one of the guys."

"Go ahead," the Chief deadpanned.

Tony sensed a shit storm looming in his immediate future but he forged ahead. "We have a bigger problem. Gavin Cross. His sleep patterns are bizarre even with our crazy shift schedules. In fact, I'm not sure he sleeps at all. He's angry. I mean, angrier than usual."

"Specifics?"

"He was going to deck me last night when the Delta fire team chopper landed."

"What set him off?"

"I told him what I observed. His hands were shaking, pupils fully dilated, and his pulse was racing."

"Did he actually take a swing at you?"

"Negative, but if I'd been anyone else, he would've flattened me."

The Chief leaned back in the swivel chair, crossed his arms over his chest, and pinned the Lead Petty Officer against the back of his seat with the O'Malley laser stare. Tony instinctively nudged the wheeled chair back a few inches. The Chief had a reputation. He was a man who would die for his men, a warrior of profound ability and experience. No one crossed him.

"You need to be damn sure about this," the Chief

said as he tipped forward in his chair. "Reports like this could end a good man's career. You sure he wasn't just testy from lack of sleep?"

Tony sucked in a deep breath and slowly exhaled. "Chief, I don't want to be that guy."

"What guy? What are you talking about?"

"The treasonous guy who gets his best friend booted off the SEAL Teams."

The Chief scowled, his tone tipped with impatience, "What aren't you saying? What other behavior have you witnessed?"

Christ. Had he screwed up reporting Gavin's behavior? Tony closed his eyes, grinding his teeth together before he answered. *Gavin was his buddy and he needed help.* Tony spoke slowly, choosing his words carefully, "Gavin sleep-walked into my room the other night experiencing a nightmare."

"How do you know it was a nightmare?"

"He drew his gun and pointed the barrel at my head."

The chief slapped his bare hand on the desk with a loud crack. "What the hell? We all sleep with loaded guns under our pillows but Cross doing something this extreme? No way. He's one mentally tough son-of-a-bitch and would never lose control."

"I agree his actions are hard to comprehend, Chief, but Gavin didn't know he was in my quarters until I spoke to him. I believe the familiarity of my voice jarred him awake. He lowered the gun. Pretended the intrusion was a prank. I demanded his weapon and he reluctantly handed it over. I engaged the safety, secured the gun, and guided him back to bed. This morning he acted like nothing happened and commented someone played a joke on him by hiding his service weapon. Chief, I swear he was in la-la land during the entire episode."

Tony heaved a sigh of relief, not at potentially ending his best friend's naval career but just for telling someone, the right someone, and getting the elephant sized weight off his chest. He understood there'd be hell to pay from Gavin and possibly some of his teammates. Among this group of men, loyalty was huge and silence was even bigger but he loved Gavin like a brother. He had to protect him. 'What goes on in the Teams, stays in the Teams.'

"I think there's a way to handle this. We don't have to go by the books."

"I'm all ears, Chief."

"Cross is one of the finest, most capable SEALs we've had on the Teams. Neither one of us wants to end his career."

"Agreed, sir," Tony nodded.

"He's participated in more successful missions than anyone else in his platoon and already has two silver stars under his belt. The Commanding Officer has him under consideration for the Medal of Honor. That's between you and me, got it?"

"Absolutely. The approval process can take years but I hope he ends up with the medal pinned on his chest. Nobody deserves the accolade more than Gavin, especially after he rescued Marine Recon from the ambush in Kumar Province."

"Yeah, he put himself smack in the middle of harm's way on that mission."

Tony added, "As he has many other times."

"So, here's the deal. I know his father had recent

heart surgery. I'm going to ask him to initiate a request for family leave for Gavin to return stateside and help run the family farm. Once he's home, Gavin will do a little R and R and get his head back into the game. We can arrange for him to see a neurologist I know and a shrink if necessary."

"You think Gavin would agree to see a doctor? He has an epic case of denial where his current problem is concerned."

"This doctor is a former SEAL Team 8 corpsman who specializes in diagnosis of PTSD and traumatic brain injury. He practices at the Naval Hospital in Jacksonville, Florida."

The persistent heaviness in Tony's chest lightened. "Sounds like he possesses the necessary credentials to get the job done."

"Let's hope so. Gavin's return to the Team hinges on correct diagnosis and thorough treatment."

"Chief, I've been to Gavin's family farm. There's nothing but acres of wide-open spaces. He'll be distraction free. After a few months, he'll be begging to get back into the action."

The Chief uncoiled from his chair and escorted Tony to the door. "That's exactly my plan.

"Round him up in a couple hours and route his ass in here. I need time to process the paperwork."

"Will do, Chief."

****

With a perfunctory double knock on the open door frame Gavin questioned, "Hey Chief, what's up? You wanted to see me?" He bunched his jaw muscles as he spoke in an attempt to disguise his apprehension at the unexpected meeting. His stomach twisted, his heart thumped against his rib cage. He tried his damnedest to project someone calm and in total control but the perspiration leaked from his armpits and he feared, seeped through his shirt. He clamped his arms tight to his side so the chief wouldn't see the wet stains.

"Have a seat, Cross," the Chief commanded as he nodded toward the chair in front of his desk. "When was the last time you talked to your Dad?" he asked, leaning forward to rest his forearms on the desk.

Gavin slipped into the chair, a puzzled look crossed his face. "Oh, I spoke to him about three weeks ago. Why?" Concern niggled the back of his mind. The last report in a recent email indicated his father's heart surgery had gone well and the recovery expected to be uncomplicated. Had his father relapsed, had a stroke or another heart attack? Guilt racked him. He should be there, taking care of his father but his sworn duty was to his men. He couldn't be in two places at once.

"Because I have a request on my desk, initiated by your father, for you to be granted emergency family leave." Poker-faced, the Chief continued, "You know I served under your old man before he retired and he's much too tough to ask for help unless he's way past needing assistance."

"What? Emergency leave? Now?" The SEAL frowned as he leaned forward placing his hands on his knees. "That's impossible. I can't leave my platoon undermanned. Removing me as point man puts the men on my team at risk." His voice rose in volume, "Don't get me wrong, Chief, I love my Dad, but there has to be another solution. He understands as a former Captain in the Navy, what duty means and my duty here is paramount."

"I'm aware of your mission schedule and recognize you and your men are stretched to the max but the Commanding Officer has already signed off on your leave. I've arranged for a temporary point man replacement. He'll arrive in two days." The Chief mellowed his tone. "Look at the situation this way, Cross. You and the team have been operating back-to-back missions for months now. The timing couldn't be better for you to take some time off."

"My head's still in the game," Gavin asserted, visibly irritated by the insinuation.

"Bottom line. Your Dad asked for help and I owe him. He saved my butt more than once."

Gavin scowled and fought his temper as the raw emotion spiked, "But..."

"No buts." The Chief cut him off. "You have your orders, Petty Officer. Pack your shit. Your bird leaves in two hours."

Chapter 2

Ariel Armstrong extracted a steak knife from the butcher-block holder and slit open the certified mail envelope stamped with a Marine Corps seal. She gulped in a breath and hesitated before removing the contents. With her brother serving in Afghanistan as a marine, official looking mail, arriving out of the blue, couldn't hold good news. As Ariel fingered the raised seal in the corner, a hot breeze swept past her, blowing strands of hair across her face. A blast of Florida summer trailed the second gust and she realized in her haste to arrive at her small one bedroom apartment and open the letter in private, she'd left her front door wide open. She slid the knife back into its opening and in a few steps, bumped the door closed with her hip.

A bottle of Riesling sat on the nearby kitchen counter. Ariel eyed its contents and decided whatever the letter revealed would go down easier with a sip or two of wine. She gingerly removed the single sheet of paper from the envelope and stuck it in the back pocket of her jeans while she poured a partial glass. Her mouth was so dry, her tongue stuck to the roof. She closed her eyes and belted down her first taste.

A silent prayer ran through her mind as she lifted the letter from her pocket and unfolded the creases. *Please God, please don't take my brother from me.* She'd skyped John last week and he'd been his usual happy-go-lucky, buffed up, handsome self. His cheerful banter with her indicated everything was routine.

She opened her eyes and read the first line, "Dear Doctor Armstrong, after several attempts to contact you by phone…" And there were the words she had dreaded. "We regret to inform you, Lt. John Armstrong has been critically injured during a combat mission in Afghanistan. He is currently in Germany for emergency treatment. As soon as he's stabilized, he'll be flown to the Naval Air Station in Jacksonville and transported to the Naval Hospital Jacksonville for further treatment…" The writing blurred as she finished reading the details.

"Damn it, no." She shouted, banging her fist on the counter top. "This can't be happening. Not after Dad. Not again." She tipped her head back but the tears streamed down her cheeks. With the letter grasped tightly in her hand she braced her back against the sink and slid down the cabinets to the floor. She couldn't suppress the chest heaves choking her breath and placed her head in her hands wondering whether her tears were from relief he survived or a dread of what they'd both face when he arrived home. "At least he's alive."

****

Ariel crawled into bed, her body weary from the wracking sobs washing over her in waves. She propped herself up on the three goose down pillows positioned against the headboard and re-read the typed words until her eyes hurt from strain, hoping she'd read them wrong but the words in the letter never changed. Her brother received spinal cord injuries during a joint operation. The last line named a Casualty Assistance Officer, Captain Jack Stern, from Camp Pendleton who had been assigned to the case. She rolled her finger over the phone number listed for support and reached for her phone. *No, not tonight. I'll call first thing tomorrow after a good night's sleep and I'm thinking straight.* She crumpled the letter and tossed the paper on the floor next to her bed. Her temples throbbed. She massaged the sides of her head. Her only sibling and single living family member jetted on his way home to an uncertain future, possibly bedridden or in a wheel chair. She didn't know.

Ariel understood better than anyone the kind of man John had become. The marines had sculpted her younger brother, an impulsive dare devil, into a disciplined soldier. One who'd resist any limitations on his physical activities? He might even reject the idea he needed her help. But she'd have his back, so he wouldn't be alone in the battle. No matter the personal cost, she'd see him through whatever came next.

A sharp beep emanated from her cell phone indicating an incoming text and jolted Ariel out of her reverie. She grabbed the phone. While she read the content of the first text, and attempted to reply, the announcement of a second message, the wording much more alarming and urgent than the first one, arrived from the same phone number. Still dressed, she rolled out of bed, slipped into her work boots, and headed for the door. "No sleep for me. It's going to be another long night," she sighed, inhaled a shaky breath, and forced the worry about her brother to the back of her mind.

****

With her foot forcing the accelerator to the floor, Ariel prayed she wouldn't be too late. Every second ticking by while she negotiated traffic on I-75 toward Ocala meant the difference between life and death...for a mare and her million-dollar foal.

She sped down the pitch-black road as the city limits of Gainesville disappeared in her rear view mirror. Ariel raised her cell phone checking the time, willing the minutes to slow somehow. The device vibrated against the palm of her hand as Dierks Bentley belted out her favorite country tune and interrupted the silence.

"Dr. Armstrong here." She answered as the first refrain of the song ended.

"Jeff Cross. Where are you right now?" His voice cracked from obvious strain.

"I'm headed down Highway 27. How's she holding up?"

"Not good. She's already down and she's been in labor far too long. She's exhausted."

"Can you see the foal's nose yet?" The doctor clamped the cell phone to her ear knowing if the answer was no, she had less than thirty minutes.

"No, I don't see a nose, just hoofs in an amniotic sack with no change in position for a long time."

"Okay, do your best to keep her calm. I'll be there in five."

"Drive careful doctor, but get here as fast as you can."

"Will do." *Yeah, right. Careful like Mario Andretti.* The obvious concern in his voice as she ended the call were the words he didn't say, "Arrive in time." His worry crept into her steely self-confidence.

The shadowy landscape blurred as Ariel stomped on the gas, lifting her foot for a few seconds as she searched for oncoming traffic at every intersection where blinking signals flashed a warning.

I haven't lost a patient yet. I'll be damned if I lose this one. The veterinarian, frustrated by the dark, narrow winding roads dominating rural Florida, slammed the heel of her palm on the steering wheel but kept her desire to flatten the pedal to the floor in check. She glanced out the window as the dark tree line whipped by, anxious about the consequences of failing. "To hell with it." She plastered her foot against the accelerator and forced the needle on the odometer further around the dial.

Sand plumed behind her truck as she maneuvered the final turn into the farm's main entrance passing under the wood-carved Wildwood Farms sign hanging between two stone pillars. Gravel flew when Ariel slammed on the brakes and slid to a stop in front of the breeding barn. She jerked the gearshift into park, checked her watch and exhaled a deep breath. "Still time."

With her medical bag clutched in her hand, she leapt out of her truck and started shouting, "Hello, I'm here," before the door could slam shut. Her voice shredded the quiet of night as her eyes scanned the area. "Where is everybody?"

Rob, the barn manager, rounded the paddock fence and yelled, "Over here." He waved the Coleman lantern he carried. "She's already down. Mr. Cross and I couldn't get her to the barn in time." In the dim light he appeared as a hobo in a dirt-covered jacket, tattered jeans, and an unshaven face. Meeting her half way he tipped his baseball cap and continued, "You know how easy going the boss usually is?"

She nodded agreement as she quickened her gait, arriving at the grassy area in three strides, where the blood bay mare lay sprawled. The moon had slipped behind a dark black cloud making the barn's two security lights and the pale yellow glow of Rob's lantern the only available illumination. Not ideal under the best of circumstances.

"Well, he's been pacing and shouting orders at me. You know Moonshine's Bandit is his prize mare and the foal is his best shot at the Derby. The future of Wildwood Farms depends upon this baby." He continued his nervous chatter. "I'm just hoping nature isn't playing a bad joke on us, since the date is April first and all."

She shot him a sideways, disbelieving stare, "You mean April Fool's Day?"

"Uh, huh." He nodded.

God, he's serious. "Rob, I can assure you superstition will not dictate tonight's outcome with this foal. Now, hold the lantern so I can get a closer look."

Ariel stepped to the rear of the horse and observed the scene before she kneeled at the mare's swollen side. Two small hooves strained against the vulva, determined to get free. "You and your baby are going to be okay, girl." She reassured the mare as she gently stroked her sweat-drenched body. Moonshine's Bandit labored to raise her head and whinnied, nudging her arm in gratitude. Ariel noticed a flicker of recognition in the soft brown eyes of the patient she called Moon and caressed her neck before angling sideways for another view of the hindquarters. The horse nickered in response and laid her head back on the damp earth with a groan.

"I don't see the head yet," she barked at Rob squatting beside her. "Get me some warm water pronto, would you?" she softened her request, dialing down the brusqueness so her own anxiety didn't seep into the already tense scene.

"On my way," Rob hoisted himself off the ground.

"Easy little lady. We'll get your baby out." She wiped the sweat off the mare's cheek and rubbed her ear with her thumb and forefinger. The horse's nostrils flared as she breathed heavily, in obvious distress. Her eyeballs rolled back in her head so only the whites were visible. A strong contraction gripped Moon's stomach muscles and intensified as the spasm rolled back along the horse's side.

Well-drilled, Doctor Armstrong spoke with certainty. "It's go time. This mare's delivering." She rolled up the right sleeve of her blue denim shirt, and then rummaged in her large plastic toolbox. With her free hand she grabbed the sterile lube and disinfectant and tossed them onto a sterile sheet situated on the ground a few inches away. She rotated sideways as Moon's anxious owner barreled toward her, towels stacked up to his chin. "I see Rob put you to work, Mr. Cross."

He dropped the pile of clean towels at the horse's head and gave her a thumb's up and a forced smile. "It's Jeff, Doctor Armstrong, and I've never been so relieved to see you." He brushed off the sweat beading on his forehead. "Do you have a prognosis yet?"

Ariel noticed him wringing his hands and adopted her calm doctor tone as she explained, "I'll have to go in and make sure the shoulders aren't lodged in the pelvic canal. With luck, the head will be tucked right on top of the legs where it's supposed to be, and if so, you can breathe easy. Everything will turn out okay."

"Here's the warm water you asked for Doc," Rob gasped as he placed the heavy bucket of water next to Ariel. "What's next?"

"Reassure Moon, keep her calm and keep her down," Ariel replied, dumping blue surgical scrub in the bucket. She twisted her head to the side, avoiding the disinfectant's potent blast as she swirled the liquid around scrubbing her hands and right arm up to the elbow.

She inserted her arm in the horse's vagina to feel for the all-important position of the two tiny hooves. *Ah, right where they're supposed to be. Fingers crossed I can feel the knees so I know the baby's not coming out backwards. Yes, these are definitely knobby little knees. With a nose resting right on top. Whew.* Relief surged through her veins. She let out the air she'd been holding in her lungs.

Jeff Cross leaned his tall muscular frame in over Ariel's shoulder. "How's it looking in there?"

She understood what he meant but Ariel couldn't help herself. She'd been so tense she couldn't ignore a little levity. "Dark," she replied, and with a conspicuous pause, continued, "and wet." She cocked her head toward the older man and grinned. As if Mother Nature wanted to join in the fun, a stream of steam suddenly rose from between the mare's legs.

His chin dimple deepened as Jeff returned the smile, "I mean do you need me to do anything?"

"Stay right where you are and be ready. I might," she grunted as she leaned in even farther and felt for any obstructions, "because this foal is super-sized."

Ariel grimaced as she withdrew her arm from the mare. "The baby's in the correct position but because of its size it seems wedged. You might have to help me pull out the baby."

"Ready and willing," he said as he rolled up his sleeves and sank to his knees next to the doctor and Rob, who continued stroking the mare's neck.

Moon whinnied frantically as Ariel clutched the foal's hooves and tugged with the next contraction. The security lights flickered as the wind picked up, obstructing what little view she had and sending her anxiety level into overdrive.

Moon lay soaked in her own sweat, exhausted from the long hours of trying to deliver the large foal on her own. The distinct chill of moisture rolled down Ariel's back soaking her shirt as she waited for the next contraction. Gritting her teeth, she studied the mare's half closed eyes and listened to her labored breathing. Time was running out. The exhausted horse was risking death from battling the forces of nature and a bigger than normal offspring. Ariel coaxed her in a soothing tone, "Just a few more pushes girl. I promise."

I need a little luck here.

As if on cue, the mare's abdominal muscles flexed, elevating her back legs several inches off the ground. Ariel leveraged her entire body weight and yanked on the tiny hooves protruding from the mare's vulva in sync with the robust contraction. The tension released like a broken spring and the familiar "whoosh" of channeled fluid filled the air as two hooves, a head, and shoulders simultaneously slid out of the mare's birth canal in one slippery slide, sending both her and the young horse sprawling onto the flattened grass. Ariel rolled to her side. The colt's lifeless body lay next to her covered in a slimy amniotic sac.

He wasn't breathing. She shoved her hand under his chest, checked for a heartbeat and felt a rhythmic thud against her fingers.

Apprehensive, Jeff leaned over them and peered at the motionless foal, "Please don't tell me he's dead. Is he alive?"

There was panic in his voice but Ariel didn't console him. Time was of the essence. "He's alive, but he's not breathing. Grab those towels and start rubbing his body. Peel off the amniotic sac as much as you can. I have to clear his airway." With her focus on the baby, she tugged her medical kit closer, retrieved a bulb syringe and after removing the sticky fluid covering his face, inserted it deeply, first into one nostril and then the other, aspirating fluid and stimulating him to breathe. "C'mon little man, breath." *Nothing.*

She dove into her bag for a shot of adrenaline, her last resort, and aimed the needle for the jugular vein when suddenly the new-born inhaled a desperate gulp of air.

"Thank God." Relief poured through Ariel as she swayed back on her heels and placed the needle in her bag. "The sooner we get the mother tending her baby the better for both of them." She grabbed one of the unused towels, wiped her face and turned her attention to the mother. The umbilical cord needed to be snipped and tied off and antiseptic applied.

Exhausted but triumphant, the mare shakily positioned her front, then her back legs and stood with a full body quiver, intent on caring for her young offspring.

Glancing over her shoulder at Jeff, Ariel's lips curved into a grin as she confirmed the obvious, "She's up. Good news just keeps coming."

Tears welled in Ariel's eyes as the baby struggled, determined to stand on its feet, anxious for food and exploration of his new world. The mare, already attentive, nuzzled him to her teat. "This is my reward," she said, dabbing the corners of her eyes with her shirtsleeve.

Each time she assisted in the miracle of birth, her career decision was reaffirmed and her years of arduous training were worth the work. She loved her job as a healer in spite of midnight emergencies and long hours. The pay wasn't too shabby, especially the free, fresh eggs, tomatoes, and country ham. A rivulet of moisture wetted her cheek. She swiped it clear and clutched the dog tags hanging around her neck. The tags were a constant reminder of her father and the sacrifice he made for his profession and his country. His memory served as inspiration for her to achieve her ultimate goal. She'd work at Calumet Farms in Lexington one day, at the top of her game and the best in her field as a neo-natal specialist. But for now, she would remain in Florida to honor a family commitment.

"Great job, Doctor," Jeff beamed. "You saved another mare with the usual nerves of steel. I don't think I've ever seen anything rattle you."

"Thanks, Jeff." Ariel kicked the sand with the toe of her boot, feigning embarrassment.

"You want to clean up a bit while Rob assists mama and baby to the barn while I fetch you a cup of coffee." He paused. "Or something a bit stronger if you like?"

"Ah, sounds great. But first, there's one more thing that requires my attention." She pointed to the back end of the mare whose placenta had partially emerged and grabbed the end, tying it off in a knot at the horse's hocks. "Rob, make sure you save the placenta in a cooler so I can examine it later. It ought to expel in an hour or so. Find me if it doesn't."

"Will do, doc." Rob grunted as he lifted the foal, scooping him by the shoulders and butt. "You're a big boy."

Ariel swiped her hands up and down her bloodstained shirt, "Let me change. I keep an extra shirt in my truck and a wee shot of whiskey in my coffee sounds like heaven." She flicked a drop of sweat from her temple as she sauntered in the opposite direction toward her truck. "See you in a few."

****

Jeff stepped into the barn and spotted Ariel leaning over the stall door watching the foal nurse. "Hi Doc. Here's your drink as ordered." He extended his arm in a gesture for her to take the beverage and observed her controlled poise in spite of the all-nighter as she swallowed a careful sip.

He took a step closer. "Listen, I've been thinking about your commute and I have an offer I want to run past you. As you know, we've finished construction on the new breeding facility and it has a two-bedroom cottage right next door to the stallion barn. We need a farm vet, someone to live on the property and manage our reproduction program. We not only have our own mares to breed every spring but we're now boarding mares from all over the South coming for our stud services. Dr. Armstrong, you're a gifted veterinarian.

I'll make it worth your while to accept the position."

"Always telling it like it is, eh Jeff?" She teased him. "I'll admit, your offer's tempting and you know how much I like working with you and the mares but I have a confession which will probably be a deal breaker, but I want you to know the truth," she blurted out, running the words together. "I come as a package deal. My brother, John is," she swallowed hard, "was stationed in Afghanistan with his Marine Recon unit. Apparently, he was badly injured during a combat mission. I don't have all the details yet but they're flying him to the Jacksonville Naval Air Station and then transporting him to the Naval Hospital for treatment. He's my responsibility now because our parents are deceased and—"

He cut her off, "God Ariel. How awful for you. Not only is the news not a deal breaker, your commitment to your brother confirms my choice. You are the right person for the job. He has served his country honorably. Paid a heavy price. Let me help."

"How?"

"We'll do what's necessary to make things accessible for him here at the farm, when he's able. Whatever he needs. Is that a yes?" Jeff grinned.

Ariel's shoulder's slumped, her head bowed. She stood silent as he witnessed her transformation from a controlled professional into what appeared to be dumbfounded surprise. Her lips parted slightly as she snagged her bottom lip with her front teeth and her arms splayed, palms up, eyes wide. "I don't know what to say."

Convinced more than ever he wanted to help, Jeff continued, "The twenty-four hour on-call might prove challenging but we can make the schedule work. And the drive to the Naval Hospital in Jacksonville is a straight shot up Highway 301 from Ocala. Not to mention, the fresh air and country living complete with a swimming pool perfect for rehab. All are complimentary components for your brother's recovery."

"And, I won't have to be around..." she hesitated, as if unsure she wanted to finish her thought, "people who are a constant reminder of how much military families sacrifice." She winced and stuck her hand out to shake. "That's a yes. Are you negotiable on the start date? I have a few things that need my immediate attention."

"Absolutely. Let's hash out the details over breakfast," he smiled as he ushered her toward the large brick farmhouse where the aroma of hickory-smoked bacon wafted into his nostrils indicating the food was already being prepared and the kitchen table most likely set by their long-term housekeeper.

Ariel sent him a curious look, "Would you still be offering me breakfast if I'd said no?"

He looked down at the well-worn path and measured his words, "Of course, but I hoped more than anything you'd say yes. I was certain the farm would be a good fit for you and your brother." Jeff probed lightly, "Has John arrived in Jacksonville yet?"

Ariel took a deep breath and let it out in a slow sigh. She raised her index finger indicating she needed a minute.

Jeff placed a hand on her shoulder. "I understand what you're going through. My son, Gavin, is a SEAL, deployed in Afghanistan. You might get a chance to meet him," he hesitated, "when his deployment ends."

Her mind spun. She had no idea Jeff had a son in the military, much less in the SEAL teams. "When will he be returning?"

Poker-faced, he answered, "He's not scheduled to be back any time soon."

****

Maybe Wildwood Farms wasn't the safe haven she'd envisioned. The last thing she wanted was to be in close proximity to an intolerable, bad-ass SEAL. Ariel especially disliked the prospect of listening to him recount the numerous conflicts in which he'd been engaged, complete with shock and awe, of course. War had an ugly face. One Ariel had personally experienced. But she was being selfish. She couldn't possibly renege on the offer now. Jeff's willingness to make the farm accessible to her and her brother was exactly what she hoped her brother needed.

"Great." She wanted to sound sincere but the only thing she cared about was not being around when his son, Gavin Cross arrived. There was plenty of time. She made a mental note to investigate alternative situations for both her and her brother before the SEAL arrived home.

****

Ariel dragged herself through the door of her apartment. It was nearly noon. Numbing exhaustion claimed her body and inhibited her satisfaction from an exceptionally mouth-watering breakfast. She dropped her gear on the floor with a thud and wandered into her bedroom. The crinkled letter remained where she'd dropped it last night. She stooped and picked up the wadded ball and smoothed the bottom section displaying the phone number. With blurry eyes, she read each numeral out loud as she punched in the number, as if speaking would help her carry out the simple task. Each ring tightened the knot in her stomach and swelled the lump in her throat. A man's voice answered in a polite tone, "Corporal Fitzpatrick. How may I help you sir or ma'am?" She stuttered, "Um, I have a letter, um…Captain Jack Stern, please."

Chapter 3

Three Weeks Later

The morning dawned sultry and hot, typical for June in Ocala, Florida, as Ariel stepped from the patio into the air-conditioned kitchen for a coffee refill. Mug in hand, she strolled to the oversized picture window in the small but tidy two-bedroom guesthouse. The rolling green hills of Ocala's thoroughbred country, stretched out before her, picturesque and peaceful. She'd finally relocated into her new home on Wildwood Farms. Perfect. Safe.

Lucky to land a job like this, even though practicing in the small town of Ocala lacked the prestige of her ultimate dream job in Lexington, Ariel was resolved her decision to stay in Florida was correct. Her ties were here, not in Lexington. She still needed those ties. Besides, Wildwood Farms had a reputation for raising some of the most beautiful and carefully bred horses in the country. As she brushed her hair into a tight ponytail, she gave herself a quick once over in the hall mirror. Jeans, boots, t-shirt, good enough for farm work, she considered, and swung open the door.

With deliberation she gripped the white banister and descended the three porch stairs one at a time while contemplating her future. "The daily choices one makes create the future," she could hear her mother saying.

"Choose wisely," drummed in her head.

Ariel figured the farm's widely respected reputation for high integrity horse breeding, in an industry sorely lacking it, outweighed the SEAL glitch. By working in Ocala she could remain close to her alma mater, The University of Florida, assist the Large Animal Division with difficult reproduction cases, and would have unlimited access to their state-of-the-art facilities. Most importantly she would still be able to oversee care for her brother and ensure he received the treatment he needed from the Naval Hospital in nearby Jacksonville.

Then, with his recovery complete, she'd fulfill her career dream of practicing at Calumet Farms in Lexington, Kentucky, the pinnacle of the thoroughbred race world. Because the demand for her specialty, equine reproduction and neo natal care, ranked number one, the opportunity would eventually present itself and Ariel planned to seize the moment when it arrived. The race world's insatiable desire for faster, stronger, record-breaking horses, created a vacuum she'd eagerly fill as a reproductive specialist.

As she sauntered to the barn, the sweet smell of fresh alfalfa hay filled her nostrils and the nickering of hungry yearlings anxious to start their day, spilled out of the barn as she strolled toward the large white sliding doors. As far as she was concerned, the newly cut hay scent smelled like heaven, better than Chanel No. 5 any day.

Her gaze flicked to an imposing male figure planted directly in her line of vision, his stance wide, wearing leather combat boots seemingly bolted to the earth. Whoever the man was, he surveyed every detail of his environment with the presence of someone whose self-confidence couldn't easily be shaken. He carried himself like he belonged here. Hell, like he owned the place. The startling combination of blue eyes, the color of glacier water, against an olive complexion and full black beard created a commanding presence. Glued like a sentry next to the man, Wager, the farm's border collie exuded absolute devotion with his tongue lolling out and head tilted up to the hand stroking him.

Jesus, who IS that dude? He can't be a new buyer interested in our foals the way Wager is fawning all over him but he's someone important, no doubt. Focus Ariel, you're here to work, not get infatuated with the first cowboy who comes along.

As if he sensed her curiosity, the enigmatic stranger turned his attention toward her. The intensity of his stare invaded her comfort zone as he coolly and completely assessed her with a visual review of her body that left her feeling undressed. The hair on her arms stood erect. She rubbed them as if removing a chill. The physical reaction was her own intuitive warning system and experience had taught her to listen to her body. She understood all too well about arrogant, possessive men. Her controlling ex-boyfriend was a moral zero and the most deceptive man she'd ever met. The image of him sent shivers skidding down her spine but she quickly thrust the memories aside. *He's out of my life and nowhere near here.*

Ariel slid the dog tags back and forth on the chain she wore around her neck, as her new boss, Jeff Cross, walked up the path toward her, wearing a face-splitting grin. He had an athletic build and in spite of suffering a recent, mild heart attack, walked with a definite stride and self-confidence in his step. The hair on his temples was streaked with gray giving him a distinguished, gentleman farmer appearance and the crow's feet around his blue eyes crinkled when he smiled.

"Doctor Armstrong, good morning. I realize you spent your first night on the property but we're anxious to put you to work." He smiled a genuine smile. "We're glad you're here."

"Thanks. It's great to be here." A sigh of relief slipped through her lips. Jeff was someone she respected and his warm demeanor told her the feeling was mutual.

Her pulse suddenly quickened as the stranger, his gaze fixated on her, advanced, moving with a noticeable athletic grace in their direction.

"Gavin, there you are. I thought you'd gone into town."

Gavin, Jeff's son, the SEAL, already here, now? What happened to, 'when his deployment is over?'

"Doctor Ariel Armstrong, I'd like you to meet my son, Gavin." Jeff wrapped his arm around the younger man's massive shoulders. "Son, this is the new vet I told you about. She's an equine specialist in high demand so I stole her away from the University of Florida and bribed her into practicing medicine here at Wildwood." He winked. "She's moved into the guest house and today is officially her first day as our in-house vet."

Steady. She stuck out her hand and looked directly into brilliant blue eyes, penetrating all the way into her bones. He only hesitated a moment before he gripped her hand in a firm handshake.

"Hello, Dr. Armstrong. So you're a specialist. A

specialist in what?"

"Reproduction." She answered, stiffening her spine as the warmth of his huge hand enveloped hers.

He cocked an eyebrow and his mouth turned up in a lazy half smile. He kept her hand in his snug clasp.

Jeez, did I just say reproduction to a man reeking of testosterone? Heat rose from her neck to her cheeks. "What I mean is we have studs flown in from all over the world for my reproductive services at the University." *This isn't getting any better.* "Your father asked me to set up a similar program here and please, call me Ariel." She snatched her hand back and tucked her thumb in the waistband of her jeans. His lips curved into a broad grin.

"I'm sure your reproductive expertise will prove to be invaluable to Wildwood Farms," he said, with a slight hint of irony in his voice.

The heat of his gaze made her light headed. In an effort to disguise her discomfort, she stuffed the thumb of her other hand in her jean's waistband and rocked on her heels.

"Now, if you'll excuse me I promised my furry friend a game of catch. Nice to meet you, Ariel. Stay out of the heat, Dad. C'mon Wager." The collie fell into step next to him as he strode down the walkway toward the barn. "We're going to play ball, buddy."

"Ariel, are you ready to see your patients?"

Jeff's smile stretched across his cheeks as he gestured toward the barn like he hadn't just dropped a flash bang in her personal space with the introduction of his SEAL son. She decided to let the newsflash go, for now and nodded, "Lead the way."

The doctor collected her rattled nerves and turned

her attention to her boss. She enjoyed watching a man in his late fifties transform into a much younger male, adding a spring to his step, when he showed off his prized horses. She jogged the few feet to catch up with his brisk pace.

A sense of accomplishment coursed through her veins as she strolled through the well-manicured rows of white stalls trimmed in hunter green. With no regrets, she sacrificed her personal life for her professional career but her mother, Abigail, had given up the most, laboring long hours in her business while raising Ariel and her brother alone. Her mother died without the opportunity to see the big pay-off but she sensed, somewhere, her mom smiled down on her.

"Ariel, is everything ok?" Jeff asked as he placed a calloused hand on her shoulder.

Suddenly aware she had mentally drifted into the past as Jeff recounted the history of his prize thoroughbreds, Ariel responded, "Oh, sorry, I'm fine Jeff." Comfortable with his avuncular manner she broached the subject pressing on her thoughts like a misstep onto a land mine. "By the way. Earlier, you said Gavin was deployed in Afghanistan? I was under the impression he wouldn't be coming home anytime soon."

Jeff studied her for a second before a frown crossed his face. "Uh, huh."

"How long is he here for," she paused, "if you don't mind me asking?"

He crooked his neck as if checking for his son's proximity to them, "No, I don't mind. Gavin was in Afghanistan with SEAL Team 2 but arrived home a few days ago. The orders rolled down the chain of command fast and unexpected for him, I think. They dictated a required extended leave but knowing Gavin, he'll do everything possible to get back in the action as soon as humanly possible. He loves this place but his heart is with the SEAL Teams."

"Oh," she took a deep breath and exhaled. "I see…"

His face softened and his mood lightened, "I want you to feel welcome. How are your living quarters? Is there anything you need so your accommodations feel more like home?"

She perceived he'd said all he wanted to on the subject of his son's leave and was changing the direction of the conversation. "The cottage is ideal. Perfect, in fact." She raised both thumbs in front of her face.

Not wanting him to feel uncomfortable, she played along but there was obviously more to Gavin's story. Guys like him didn't get assigned leave and come home for no reason.

She added, "I wanted to thank you for installing the handicapped ramp next to my porch stairs for John. I also noticed you put handrails in the shower so he can go in on his own. You know, he prides himself on his independence." Her voice cracked as she simultaneously gazed down at her feet. "He always has." This wasn't an easy subject for her to talk about. In fact, facing the truth of her beloved baby brother paralyzed from a Humvee landing on top of him in an IED explosion, ripped her heart out. "You've taken care of everything. I can't thank you enough."

"Honestly, the upgrades were simple but you're welcome." He grinned warmly, squeezing her arm.

"When John finishes up his rehab at the Naval Hospital his quarters will be ready for him."

Ariel peeked out the sliding barn door. She gasped out loud as she spotted what had to be the picture of horse breeding perfection. A young filly galloping across the paddock with tail flying straight out behind her appeared to be on a collision course with the fence and the two of them. The young horse's ebony coat glistened and a jagged blaze across her forehead appeared stamped on by a strike of silver lightning. Long white stocking legs pumped up and down with the kind of startling speed Ariel had rarely witnessed. Her heart leapt at the vision. This filly exuded an overload of attitude and stamina in abundance as she tossed her slender head and emitted a shrill whinny in her charge up to the fence. Ariel's cheeks flushed as what would be any horse farm's most prized possession stretched across the top of the fence and nuzzled her neck.

"Nike is her name," Jeff explained. "From Greek mythology, 'the winged goddess of victory.' Her sire is descended from Affirmed and her dam is Rebel Victory, the best brood mare we've ever had here at Wildwood Farms."

Ariel climbed up on the bottom rung of the wooden fence and kissed the velvet nose while she fondled the long, elegant neck extended over the fence. "Where have you been all my life," she cooed.

Jeff smiled with satisfaction. "Gavin brought the mare and her foal back from a neighboring farm this morning where I stashed them while we upgraded the breeding facilities. Professional opinion, Doc?"

As her fingertips made contact, Nike squealed and pawed the dirt feverishly. The doctor hadn't connected and been this excited over a horse in a long time. Ariel leaned forward and Nike brushed a feather light kiss on her cheek. "She's flawless."

****

Gavin turned the corner of the barn and witnessed the most precocious filly in his father's stable nuzzling the new doctor. *Is this for real?* Nike was the terror of the barn, nipping, charging, and generally instilling fear into anyone who handled her. Her current behavior was no less than amazing to him. His father stood nearby looking almost giddy, as he beheld the obvious instant bond between the smitten doctor and a normally unruly filly.

No one had a way with strong-headed horses like Gavin did—until now. His gaze stayed fixed while he forced his heart out of his throat. He observed woman and horse together and stood witness to a rare ritual in beauty. A blue ribbon filly and a stunning woman drawn together in some sort of ancient, mystical union filled him with an uncomfortable warmth and contentment in his gut. He cautioned himself not to become too intrigued with the new doctor. She had the poised demeanor of a girl with a string of boyfriends, a rich, pampered kid whose parents never said no to her. Shit, she probably drove a Beemer. The fragile hand he'd shaken earlier had been too small and free of calluses from hard work. He doubted she had the constitution to hold up under real farm labor. Nope, she'd be trouble in his screwed up, complicated life. Best to back away.

A deep-throated growl ripped Gavin's attention from the doctor. He turned in time to see Wager lunge and collide mid-air with a three-four foot rattlesnake aiming his strike for Gavin. Instead, the snake sank its fangs into the dog's front paw injecting deadly venom before recoiling for another hit.

Wager yelped in pain. Gavin's survival instincts soared into overdrive. He grabbed the closest weapon, a mucking shovel, and raising the handle high over his head brought the curved surface down on the viper, over and over until the snake lay smashed to a pulp. Wager limped over to his master, whimpered and lifted his paw. Gavin knelt and eased him to the ground. In one easy motion, he whipped his belt off, and yanked his KA-Bar knife from its leather holster. He straddled the dog and snugged the belt around Wager's thigh, creating a tourniquet. Bending closer beside Wager he lowered the tip of the blade to the fang marks, poised to cut and suck the venom out before it could spread. "It's okay, boy." His voice soothed.

Ariel dashed across the clearing and screamed, "No, don't use the knife. Remove the tourniquet." She shoved him aside, knocking him off balance.

Pissed she kicked him out of the way, he shouted, "Hey, what the fuck do you think you're doing?" and deftly stepped back into position, his eyes narrowed. She glared at him and with controlled calm ordered, "Go get my truck. It's parked right behind the barn. I need my medical bag," Ariel tossed the keys in his direction and returned her concentration to Wager. The dog's eyes drooped, his tongue lolled out the side of his mouth and he panted heavily. She loosened the belt around Wager's leg.

"Do you have anti-venom in the truck?"

"No, I don't carry anti-venom." She met his hard look evenly with her own, "The first two hours are critical and we're losing precious time." He stared at her transfixed. "Why are you still here? *Go*. Now. Get the truck."

As Gavin scrambled to his feet, Ariel yelled for his father to call the University of Florida Vet School emergency number. He sprinted over to her truck. *Why the hell didn't she carry anti-venom? What kind of dumb ass vet works in the country and doesn't stock snake anti-venom?* He fought his anger and the avalanche of aggression bearing down on him. As adrenaline flooded his system and his pulse thundered in his neck, he struggled for control. On the battlefield he channeled these emotions to stay alive but lashing out at the doctor wasn't going to help his dog, now in a fight for his life. And it was his fault. His lapse in situational awareness resulted in Wager suffering venom intended for him. He yanked open the driver's door of Ariel's truck, cranked the engine and shoved the gear in reverse, backing the vehicle to Ariel and Wager.

"Gavin, grab a saddle blanket from the truck bed and help me transfer Wager into the front seat," she said. "We need to keep him stable." Pitching forward, her hands supporting Wager's head, she stood as Gavin ducked his hands under the dog's rear and helped her climb into the truck. He placed the dog on her lap and handed her the black medical bag she'd requested.

"You drive while I phone the doctor on call in the emergency room so they have the anti-venom ready," she said, digging into the contents of her bag.

Gavin stretched across the seat and petted the dog's motionless tail. Wager shivered from poison trickling into his bloodstream. A sense of dread washed over

Gavin as he tucked the blanket tighter around the collie's belly. "Is he going to make it?"

"He'll make it." Ariel said, her voice emphatic. "I'll start treatment. You haul ass."

Both hands gripped the wheel as Gavin stepped on the gas, sending the truck like a bullet out of the driveway, fishtailing on the gravel road. Once he merged onto the interstate, he opened up the high-performance V8 engine. Screw getting a speeding ticket…he had to get Wager to the hospital in time to save his life. He weaved in and out of traffic, honking his horn, warning slower drivers to get out of the way. Ariel, unlike most women who rode with him, didn't white-knuckle the armrest. Instead, she soothed and calmed Wager. The coo of her voice put his dog totally at ease. He glanced out of the corner of his eye as she prepared a hypodermic needle and plunged the point deep into Wager's shoulder. "What are you giving him?"

"Benadryl. It'll buy us some time and hopefully prevent tissue damage." She methodically prepared the second shot and offered, "An anti-inflammatory."

The third and final injection followed without comment so he asked, "What are you giving him now?"

"Powerful antibiotics." Carefully, lovingly, she eased the heavy horse blanket back over the dog without a glance in his direction.

As Wager's labored breathing deepened, Gavin's grip on the wheel tightened. All he could do was drive and hope the dog wouldn't succumb to the pervasive poison.

****

The night dragged on, minute by excruciating

minute, especially with the marked lack of conversation. Not that she was interested in talking to Captain America. Accustomed to sleep deprivation, she didn't need his company to stay awake.

Navy SEAL or not, she couldn't deny a certain amount of respect for Gavin's devotion to Wager. Even though he was doing what every dog lover would do, she somehow believed a hard, rough man like Gavin lacked a softer side.

Throughout the afternoon and into the evening, Gavin dozed through half-closed eyelids. It was no mystery how he'd gotten his muscled, well-toned physique. SEAL training was a bitch, but it appeared well worth the effort from where she was sitting. Man, oh man did he look…fit. And face it, hot. She checked out the definition in her own legs, twisting from side to side, as she scanned the flexed muscles. In top condition, she recognized being fit was a necessary component to her job as well. She once took a farrier course at her adviser's insistence, which turned out beneficial for a multitude of reasons. Not only could she shoe a horse but she was also capable of treating foot related ailments without a specialist. With work like hers, who needs a gym? Try heaving an anvil in and out of your truck.

Ariel wanted this to end well for Wager. She liked happy endings although the reality existed she couldn't save every animal. This was her life, not some Hollywood version acted out on the silver screen. She drifted half in, half out of sleep. It wasn't simply her job; it was her passion, her purpose to heal as many animals as she could.

Her attention traveled back to Gavin as sleep

threatened to drag her under. What a face. Rugged and tanned with a straight nose and the most sensuous lips she'd ever seen. His dark almost black hair, although short, was thick and rich, begging to have fingers dragged through it. His tightly muscled body stretched out in front of her with such masculine perfection. He reminded her of a highland warrior, both hands swinging his claymore, slicing through his enemies with the two-edged blade. Cobalt blue eyes...

Ariel jerked awake at the sound of her phone's alarm. She checked the time. Six A.M. Stiff from sleep, curled up on the waiting room sofa she sat up, stretched, and remembered the dream she'd had. Crap. What the hell had she been fantasizing? Get over it. This man's not for you. Face it. He acts as though he doesn't even like you.

The attending vet ambled through the door from the intensive care unit and nodded to Ariel. She smiled back, relieved as Wager followed behind and in spite of his bandaged foot and slight limp, made a beeline for his owner. Gavin met him on the floor, buried his face in Wager's neck and careful of his paw, hugged him. Wager covered Gavin's face in long hearty licks. Right now she wouldn't mind being Wager. She imagined what those hands might feel like on her. Surprised at her digression, she hoped Gavin couldn't read her provocative thoughts.

"How's the patient?" He asked, his voice low and husky, as he ran his hands in a loving sweep along Wager's side.

She struggled to reconcile her ambivalence toward this angry, tougher-than-nails man as he affectionately caressed his dog. His show of tenderness ignited heat in her suntanned cheeks, flooding them with pink. Maybe she'd been wrong about him...

"He's out of the woods for the most part," the attending doctor answered. "His eyes are clear and the swelling is down. He'll be up and tagging along behind you soon enough but..."

Gavin scowled, "But what?" Ariel and the emergency vet exchanged a knowing glance, indicating they both understood the nervous reaction of a concerned owner, before the doctor initiated his response. "Normally, we'd have to monitor him here in the hospital for a week, but if Dr. Armstrong will agree to observe him at the farm, we can release him today. She can administer the required ten day antibiotic and anti-inflammatory twice a day from his home."

With his attention directed to Ariel, Gavin stroked and petted his dog. "All right with you, Doc?"

"Absolutely. It would be my pleasure."

"He's in excellent hands, Mr. Cross." The attending vet nodded toward Ariel and smiled as he shook hands with Gavin before heading back into the intensive care unit.

Ariel reasoned, "It would be better for Wager if..."

"No clarification necessary." Gavin cut off her explanation as he peered into her dark, soulful eyes. He placed his hands on her shoulders. "I understand and thanks. I really mean it, Ariel." He leaned in closer and placed his right hand over his heart. "Thank you."

Waves of hot emotion overwhelmed her. "You're welcome." Uncomfortable, she instinctively stepped back. He was way too close. No matter how good he looked on the outside or how he made her feel, this was not the man for her.

"Wait. I really meant it when I said thank you." He wrapped his arms around her and curled her into his body.

She returned the hug. The show of affection registered as gratefulness not as a flirtation, so no problem. Wager had survived.

He tilted back and searched her face. The tension in the air changed to a palatable desire. His eyes dropped to her mouth and he kissed her softly curving lips, devouring every inch as he coaxed his tongue inside.

She tasted his hunger and returned the kiss, tangling her tongue with his. Electric waves warmed her belly as her desire ballooned and all rational thought deserted her. She massaged her body into him and deepened the kiss forgetting...they were in the very public, university emergency waiting room. *OMG*. She jerked free and quickly wiped her mouth, hoping to erase any evidence of her lapse in judgement. She glared up at him, stunned at how quickly things had gotten out of control.

"Ariel...I, uh..." As he fumbled for words, his voice cracked.

"I did this for Wager, not you." She blurted, desperate to retreat before one of her colleagues witnessed her looking all hot and bothered. Without a backward glance, she turned on her heel and shoved through the double exit doors.

Chapter 4

Gavin's heart stuck in his throat as she exited, head tilted back in indignation, the metal tack in her boot heel tapping staccato defiance. She disappeared through the perpetual, swinging doors of the waiting room. His emotions swung between regret over his impulsiveness and a desire for another taste. He hadn't expected to kiss her.

What was I thinking?

"It was merely gratitude for saving you, fella." Wager's tail thumped in eager agreement. "A little kiss." He petted the dog's head. "Just a kick-ass little kiss." Wager cocked his head as Gavin knelt on one knee and stroked him while he talked, "But man, was she pissed. Damn. For a minute there I'd swear she enjoyed the kiss as much as I did. I'd better go find her and apologize…for Dad's sake."

Jeff Cross appeared in the waiting room doorway, his brows furrowed. "Gavin, how's our boy?"

"Oh, hi Dad. I didn't see you come in? He's not quite ready to hunt rabbits yet but Wager's tough as nails. He'll be chasing me around the barn in a week or two. No doubt about it."

"Glad to hear it. And you? I bet it was a long night crumpled up on an uncomfortable waiting room sofa."

"Combat naps." He stretched his powerful arms over his head. "I'm an expert after sleeping in flea-infested sand and rock for six months. So the waiting room was like the Hilton—sort of." He half-smiled as he recognized the curious expression on his father's face and knew more questions were coming. Gavin relaxed his shoulders and waited but Jeff simply grabbed his son's upper arm, squeezed and turned to leave. Then he stopped mid-step, did an about face and spoke, almost sheepishly.

"Ariel drove out of the parking lot at demon-chasing speed. Then I walk in here and you're mumbling to yourself. Anything you want to tell your old man?"

"Yeah, I was talking to *Wager*." He crossed his arms. "And I'm glad she doesn't drive a BMW." *Am I making any sense?*

Gavin fidgeted, a younger version of himself caught playing with fire, as his father chuckled and uttered an, "uh-huh."

Damn, he reads me like a book.

As a teenager there was no getting past his Dad's keen eye and apparent omnipresence. Granted there hadn't been much time to raise ever-living hell on a seven hundred acre horse farm but he'd given it his best shot.

Honesty is the best policy. "I kissed her and made a colossal mistake."

"I knew it." Jeff laughed.

"What's so funny?" he asked, his voice tinged with sarcasm.

"Oh, call it a hunch but I suspect most men find Ariel's stunning looks appealing. Of course, the fact she's smart, accomplished, and nice as hell doesn't hurt."

Gavin realized the old man was enjoying baiting him and willed his defensive tone to cease. "I kissed her as a thank you for helping Wager. It was a meaningless little kiss but she took it all wrong. In fact, the next time I see her I'll apologize."

"Why do you need to apologize if it was a meaningless little kiss? And why would you think kissing her was a mistake?"

"Never mind." He had no reason to be angry, except with himself, but the tension continued to tick in his jaw. "Do you know where she went?"

"She got an emergency call and flew out of here to a llama farm north of Gainesville."

"Did you say llama farm?"

"Yeah, a couple of punks used golf clubs and vented their rage on two llamas, a mother and her baby. She didn't have time for details but the beating sounded awful." Gavin viewed the grim look on his father's face and replied, disgust in his voice, "Assholes, Dad, cold, calculating assholes. I don't envy Ariel as the responder on this call."

"Me either but she's a trooper."

"Agreed. By the way, your goading worked, as usual."

"Oh yeah, how?" his father questioned.

"I spilled my guts about kissing Ariel." No longer peeved, he teased and pointed his finger. "I enjoyed kissing her. Gotta go." He spun on his heel and stopped, rubbing his chin, "I don't have a car."

Obviously amused at his son's distracted behavior, Jeff smiled. "You can drive mine. I'll call Rob to fetch me."

"You sure? I can wait here for Rob."

"No, you need to get Wager home. I have phone calls to return and can get them done here without distraction." Gavin nodded and proceeded toward the exit calling out over his shoulder, "After I drop off Wager, I have some errands to run." *I have a sneaky feeling Ariel will need 'an after llama rescue beer' in a few hours.*

****

Late in the afternoon, after Wager was settled and comfortable at home, Gavin climbed into his jeep and headed for Gainesville. He formulated his strategy for approaching Ariel as he traveled I-75. But unlike what he told his father he had no real plan to apologize. In fact, if he was honest with himself what he wanted to do was kiss her again.

The kudzu-covered trees lining the country road ended abruptly as he merged onto the interstate. The miles slipped by as he drove at a steady speed and mulled over the problem of how to proceed with Ariel. He would use his Caveman charm, direct and blunt. He slowed and flicked the jeep's turn signal as he peered down the Archer Road exit, the main stretch into Gainesville. He mentally recounted his past here. Still flooded with college traffic, college students, and college everything including the primary University of Florida symbol, the gator, Archer Street was the same as it had been a decade ago. *But I've changed. God, how I've changed.*

A few months ago he recalled how he popped the ripcord on his chute and sailed unnoticed along with twenty of the world's best Special Warfare Operators into the midnight sky over Afghanistan.

From the moment he taped his clanking plastic

canteen to his thigh in the hull of the C-130 aircraft, Gavin accepted the fact he might not survive the mission, but he lived for the exhilaration of the wind whipping by his body as he swooped through the sky at one hundred twenty miles per hour. The adrenaline rush of executing death defying feats on a daily basis where he controlled the outcome drove his competitive spirit. A career in Naval Special Warfare was not for the weak and faint-hearted. It was a discipline full of risk and hazard but there was no turning back for him. The SEAL had found his mission in life.

A horn blared behind the slow-moving jeep jarring Gavin back to the present.

"Someone obviously passed out on the car horn," he mumbled to himself.

Damn, what am I doing? This is exactly why I can't get emotionally involved with the opposite sex, most especially with a woman like Ariel. She'd be a big distraction. Make it M-A-J-O-R. Something I can't afford right now.

Gavin nimbly whipped the car around and turned down University Avenue looking for the familiar black and white cow print adorning the outside of his favorite bar, Eight Seconds.

Just a tall, cold one and I'll head home.

The familiar drawl of Tim McGraw filled the air as Gavin punched start on his CD player. He sang about setting his circus down and Gavin lustily followed along, belting out each line like a pro. The jeep rolled into the back parking lot just as the singer finished his tribute. Gavin slowed the vehicle to a crawl as he scanned for empty spaces and listened to the ear-numbing crunch of gravel.

What the hell? He squinted in the twilight.

A stocky, dark male stooped beside a white Ford pick-up. It looked like Ariel's truck, same model, year…

The glint of silver twisted in the man's hand. Gavin leaned out the driver's side window for a better look.

Holy Shit. He's keying her truck.

In one fluid motion Gavin yanked the gearshift into park, opened the door and hit the ground at a dead run, exploding onto the scene. He slammed into the hunched-over man and knocked him face down into the gravel. Gavin snatched the keys from the perpetrator's clutched fist. In a second swift grab, he gripped the back of the man's collar and hauled him up for inspection.

The stranger cupped blood in his palm and yelled, "You broke my nose."

"Tough," Gavin growled. "You're lucky your nose is all I broke, so far. Don't you know it's not nice to key cars?" He pictured his fist smashed into the guy's sneer but fought to tamp down the surging anger.

"What's your name, asshole?" Gavin tightened his grip on the man's collar.

He didn't answer but flailed his arms as he fought to free himself from Gavin's iron grip.

The blast of police sirens averted the men's attention as flashing blue strobe lights beamed into view. Nosy bar customers streamed out and added to the confusion.

Partially blinded by the headlights of the first police car on the scene, Gavin couldn't see the leggy female who approached. But oh, he could sense her as she stomped up and looked right through him to his hostage.

"Drake," Ariel fumed, her hands fisted, "What the hell are you doing here?"

In the light provided by the police car, Gavin skimmed her sheet-white face and eyes-wide stare. He recognized fear from studying the faces of young soldiers in their first firefight and this lady telegraphed spooked.

"The little weasel keyed your truck." Gavin jumped in, gazing at her luscious mouth. The soft, sweet lips he'd kissed earlier were quivering. She bit her bottom lip and swiped her hands on her pants as if ridding herself of unwanted dirt. He sensed her tough-it-out determination and withheld the urge to fold her into his arms. Instead, he placed his body as a barrier between her and Mr. Numb-nuts.

A young, attractive woman stepped forward from the crowd, put her arm around Ariel's waist and comforted her, "Ariel, are you okay?"

"Yeah, Sierra, I'm okay."

Gavin gave a quick nod to the female and turned to the first policeman who arrived on the scene.

"Officer, this man should be arrested. I'm sure Dr. Armstrong wants to press charges."

"I already have," Ariel stated. She grabbed the dog tags around her neck and tugged them back and forth.

"You want to explain what's going on?" Concern painted on his face, Gavin bent eye level to Ariel.

Silent, she shook her head back and forth, still gripping the tags in her fist.

Sierra spoke to the police officer, "He's violating a restraining order." She faced Gavin and arched an eyebrow, offering a non-verbal explanation.

The officer placed his hand on the butt of his gun as his squinted gaze raked over the man secured in front of him, "I need a picture ID, please." Nodding at Gavin, "Sir, you can release him, now."

"This guy broke my nose, officer. You need to arrest him," Drake whined and flipped his thumb at Gavin.

Unsympathetic, the officer repeated, "Picture ID, sir."

Drake produced his driver's license and reluctantly handed it to the police officer. "Wait here," the officer said flatly and returned to his cruiser.

A second police cruiser skidded to a stop next to the first car. A beefy cop got out, walked over to the first police officer and started a quiet conversation. After a couple of minutes he wandered over and addressed Gavin, "We verified the information. I'll take him off your hands as soon as I snap some pictures of the truck's damage."

He turned to both women and said, "Ladies, we're all set here. He's leaving with us."

Gavin wrapped his arm around Ariel's shoulders and gently coaxed her toward the scarred truck. "You want me to follow you back to the farm? Or, leave your truck here and ride home with me?"

Her body sagged. "Thanks, but I'm staying at Sierra's tonight. I can leave my truck at a local repair shop to get fixed and lease a rental. Don't worry. I'll drop anchor at the farm early tomorrow, probably before you're up."

Snick, snick, snick... Without turning around Gavin recognized the sound of locked metal handcuffs and visualized the police officer scrunching Drake's head down as the scumbag ducked under the doorframe of the police car and onto the back seat.

"All right." He didn't pursue the point. Ariel obviously wasn't prepared for the relentless stream of questions percolating in his mind. "See you tomorrow." He nodded good night to both women.

What in God's name is going on here? With the asshole in custody Ariel's probably not in imminent danger but he needed to get to the bottom of this cluster-fuck. No way will this crap spill over to the farm.

He'd get to the bottom of it. He definitely would. Interrogation, Special Forces style, wouldn't work and wasn't needed on the skittish doctor. She'd require finesse and a gentle touch to reveal the truth and he was more than willing to offer as much "comfort" as she could take.

Chapter 5

Damn strange, Gavin thought as he recalled Ariel's exit. Without uttering a single syllable to him, she had climbed into her scarred truck and eased out of the parking lot. The question now was whether or not to tell his father about the incident. As far as his dad was concerned she walked on water; at least with respect to horses, she did. The new breeding program was important for the future of the farm. His Dad had tagged Ariel as the woman for the job. It meant a lot to anyone who crossed paths with Jeff Cross, the most deliberate man he'd ever known.

No, he'd wait until he had more information, like where she got those dog tags. He hadn't noticed them before but the way she clung to them, as though they were a life preserver in a stormy sea, meant something. There was no mention she'd been in the military when his Dad gave him the low down on her credentials. In retrospect, there was no mention of anything about her personal life, certainly not a sleaze-bag ex-boyfriend.

Gavin hopped back in his jeep and headed for the interstate. And home. He needed thinking time to wrap his wits around the recent detour in his career. The paperwork for his unrequested leave flew up and down the flag pole and the next thing he knew, the ramp of a C-130 cargo plane rolled down and Tony, the SEAL team corpsman, shoved him on board, smiling and waving goodbye like Gavin was headed for an island vacation. What was that all about? Something didn't add up but not one of his teammates would tell him what the hell was going on. Tony insisted the trip home was about R&R and helping his father recover from heart surgery. Shit, they all needed R&R. The last mission was a ball buster but wasn't ball busting their specialty? He could hear Mr. "go with the flow" Tony convincing him to board the C-130, "C'mon Caveman, take some time, go check in on your Dad and the farm. Get a little extra snooze, drink a few brews, relax, and don't forget to stay classy. Enjoy the view, man." Oh yeah, the joke's on them 'cause he was definitely enjoying the view but the landscape had nothing to do with it. A certain tall, sassy, ponytailed doctor dominated the scenery in his mind's eye. Smiling he put the day's events behind him and imagined lining up the empty plastic water jugs on the fence posts in the back pasture, mentally taking aim at each one, rapid fire. The hail of bullets from a little target practice was exactly what he needed to soothe the savage beast roaring inside him. Tomorrow promised to be a good day.

****

The sun barely breached the horizon when Gavin rolled out of bed, tossed on his cargo pants and t-shirt, and laced up his work boots. He stooped to unlock the safe, which secured his service weapon, and checked to ensure the gun's chamber had been emptied last night before sliding it into the holster on his hip. His duffle bag, loaded with boxes of ammo, as well as ear and eye protection, was zipped shut and ready to go.

His stomach growled. *Breakfast would be nice.* He flipped off the light in his room and closed the door behind him. The aroma of bacon frying and coffee brewing wafted up the stairs quickening his rush to get to the bottom.

"Something smells ready for me to eat," he said to the housekeeper, sneaking a piece of bacon she was blotting with a paper towel.

"Hold your horses, young man." She smacked his hand. "Go fix yourself a cup of coffee and give me five minutes. I'll scramble some eggs to eat along with the bacon."

"Bessie Mae, you're too good to me." He kissed her cheek while his hand snaked around her back for another taste of pork.

"What? You think I'm blind? I saw you." She grinned, showing off her dimpled cheeks. "You're still a bottomless pit, just like you were as a teenager except you didn't have black fuzz all over your face. Go shave."

Hiring Bessie Mae was the only positive result from his mother's death. She took charge of the household her first day and allowed them to grieve.

"I'm a growing boy," he teased. "And no way am I shaving this off. I'll need it when I go back on active duty," he said, stroking his beard.

"Whatever you say." She rolled her eyes. "Sit. Eat. Then out of my hair." She placed a plate full of eggs, bacon, and a thermos of steaming coffee on the breakfast table.

Gavin laughed, "Yes ma'am."

****

The drive from the family farmhouse to the remote pasture he used for target practice lasted a brief five minutes.

Gavin mentally cycled through the events of yesterday, pasting invisible sticky notes in his head, until the road dead-ended at the pasture gate. He slid out of his jeep, grabbed his gear, and headed for his favorite shooting spot over the knoll. As he started his ascent up the hill, a series of muted muffled cracks jolted him and he changed his casual gait to a fast jog. "Who the hell is shooting on my property?" he cursed as he automatically unsnapped the holster and drew his gun. With a magazine already loaded in the grip, he attained the top of the hill, ready for action if necessary.

Holy Shit. It's Ariel. In an attempt to get her attention without surprising her, Gavin cupped his hands around his mouth and yelled, "Cease fire, cease fire."

He stepped from behind a giant oak tree waving his arms. He could see she was fully equipped, armed with her 'wake me up smiling' body and…her weapon. She holstered her gun, nodded, and started up the hill in his direction.

As she approached, hips casually swinging, hand outstretched to shake his, the breeze caught her jacket, blowing it back an inch, exposing the holstered, clip in, 9mm handgun. His hand auto-extended to grasp hers; his brain too busy single tasking, *the woman's packing*, to process anything else.

He smiled as he shook her hand, putting on his 'everything's cool face.' "Hi Doc, I didn't know you liked shooting, uh, I mean, guns."

"Yeah, you never know what kind of critters you might encounter out here in the back pasture," she joked and exaggerated a wink.

He didn't miss the playful dig but disarmed by her

beauty, his gaze fixated on her perfectly symmetrical face. When he finally spoke, his hard stare turned soulful in an attempt to apologize, deciding it was the right thing to do after all. "Hey, about yesterday, I might have over reacted a bit with my hair missile so close to death."

"Did you just call Wager a hair missile?" She straightened her spine and squared her shoulders. "God, you and your military lingo crap. He's a dog, not a missile, for Pete's sake. You are not in a war zone in spite of the fact you have," she stepped in closer eyeballing the gun, "an enormous pistol strapped to your thigh."

Gavin couldn't help himself. Before she had a chance to retreat, he grabbed her arms and zeroed in on her pouty mouth until they made contact. Her lips tasted warm and wet with a hint of coffee. He expected her to resist but she parted them allowing him to thrust his tongue deep into every corner of her mouth. As Gavin savored the intimacy, Ariel unstrapped her gun belt and dropped it to the ground. He helped her shrug out of her jacket and deepened his kiss, basking in the connection with her luscious lips. She flattened her body against his, rubbing up and down his arms while she squirmed against his crotch. Her long leg encircled his thigh and her breasts thrust into his hard chest. His heart slammed against his rib cage as he placed both hands on either side of her soft round bottom and lifted her legs around his waist. He glanced nearby for the closest tree and in two long strides pinned her against the trunk of a hundred year old oak. Gavin nuzzled his erection into her abdomen making his intentions clear. In too deep to stop, he buried his nose in her thick, honey colored hair and inhaled a smell of fresh apricots and cream. He wanted her, all of her, right now.

Ariel quivered, wove her fingers behind Gavin's neck, and yanked him to her.

An intense hunger gripped his crotch as his warm breath caressed her lips.

"This is a mistake," she muttered, a note of frustration in her voice. "Even though my hormones are screaming, go, go, go."

Gavin held fast to her arms, ignoring her utterance as he stared at her hardening nipples, "Your body disagrees."

She let out a breathy reply, "My lapse in judgment will come back to bite me…"

He interrupted her protest by palming her breasts and massaging each one in a lazy circular motion. Her nipples responded and stood erect begging to be stroked.

She leaned back slightly as she simultaneously grabbed his web belt and yanked. "This needs to go." It popped open allowing her access to the few buttons below. She smiled up at him through half-closed eyes.

A shit-eating grin spread across his face. "I like seeing you so turned on."

"On fire is more like it," she quipped. "Any more foreplay and I'm a goner."

"Then, let's cease with the foreplay." He meandered his hand under her shirt and unhooked the clasp of her bra.

She gasped, flattening her back against the tree and pinning his hand. "We need protection. I don't have any. Do you?"

Exasperated, he patted his jeans pockets. "My

wallet's in the jeep and I don't carry condoms in my gun case."

With her bra strap dangling down her back, she splayed her hands flat against his chest and leaned back. "We can't do this right now. I have to go."

"What?" He vigorously shook his head, confused by the change in momentum.

"Now," she peeled her legs off his hips hitting the ground with a thump.

Dumbfounded, he attempted to regain his focus. "Why? What's really wrong?"

"I'm not ready, we're unprepared, and you're missing a little foil package," she declared, visually coercing his grip off her arms.

He didn't want to let go but released his snug hold. Ariel was correct. The one time he left his wallet in the jeep, he needed its contents.

"You're right and I'm insane for storing my wallet in the jeep but there are other ways to enjoy each other." His lips turned up in a salacious smile.

Ariel shivered. "I'm not saying this wasn't fun but I'm in uncharted waters here. I don't really know you."

Gavin ran his thumbnail down her arm. "Well, we can remedy how well we know each other right now."

"I'll bet," she replied gazing at his wandering thumb.

"We do need to have a chat about the episode in the bar parking lot. I have questions and I'll bet you have answers," he acquiesced, needing to keep his lust for the doctor in check...for now.

"Later," she replied, picking up her jacket and gun belt. In an about face, she headed down the hill toward her truck. When she leveled out at the bottom, she looked back at him with an ambivalent stare and raised her hand in a mock salute. Then she jumped in her rented truck and sped off.

Chapter 6

"Hey Sierra, it's me again. Can you talk?" Ariel leaned in the front door of her best friend's house, inhaling the smell of fresh brewed coffee and sandalwood candles. She had to tell someone what happened before she exploded and Sierra Sanchez was always her trusted first choice. Ariel loved Sierra like a sister. They had played volleyball on the high school team and shared an apartment in college. While she attended vet school, Sierra enrolled in law school at the same university. They were allies in everything and always would be.

"Sure thing R, come on in. Twice in one week? What gives?" Sierra ushered her unexpected guest through the tiled foyer and with a wave of her hand indicated she should grab one of the two stools at the kitchen bar. "Can I get you something to drink? Ice tea? Coffee?"

"Water." She smacked her lips. "Thanks, I'm a little parched."

"Hey, aren't you supposed to be working? You left before dawn this morning or at least I think you did because I was still sleeping, like most sane people." Sierra chuckled as she leaned into the opened door of the refrigerator and retrieved a bottle of water. "Here you go."

"Thanks. I already did my rounds and took the

afternoon off. Which is why I went shooting and why I'm in trouble and OMG, I did something I swore I'd never do, well, not anytime so soon anyway." Ariel gushed as she plopped down on the cushioned seat.

"Oh jeez, you entered a wet t-shirt contest?" Sierra giggled and claimed the chair next to her, wrapping a strand of her naturally curly brunette hair around her index finger.

"Very funny. I did something so good and so bad, both at the same time. I don't know how to feel." She flung her hands in the air.

"Sorry Ariel, but you are straight as an arrow and not prone to getting semi-naked in front of strangers so I'm trying to imagine the wildest thing you could have done. But, I gotta admit, I've never seen you so frazzled."

"I need some feedback on what happened. Another point of view." With her fingers an inch apart she showed her friend how narrowly she missed a close call. "I was this far from having incredibly hot sex with my boss's son under a tree in a pasture." The words poured out in a forced breath as if saying it fast would minimize the impact. *Silence...uh oh.* "Sierra? Say something."

"Ahhhh. Now that's what I'm talking about." Sierra bit her upper lip in an attempt to hold back a grin, accentuating the dimple in her chin. The smile defied her and spread ear to ear as she continued, "Under a tree, on the grass, did you get bare naked before stopping the action? Tell me everything, all of it."

Goaded by her best friend, she inhaled a breath and spat out, "Up against a very large oak tree. Almost."

Her attempts at restraint failed. Sierra couldn't hold back and started laughing, her jumble of dark curls bounced around her perfectly oval face.

Ariel stared dumbfounded as Sierra's shoulders shook from uncontrolled laughter. "What the hell, Sierra. This is serious. I almost had sex with, well, you know, with a very friggin' hot guy, a virtual stranger, the guy from last night at Eight Seconds bar."

"OMG, girlfriend. The hunk with the pale blue eyes and pirate beard is your boss's son?"

"Ohhhh, yes. Gavin Cross, the one and only offspring of Jeff Cross, my employer."

"Now all his protectiveness toward you makes sense. I didn't bring up any hot topics last night because I figured you didn't need the extra drama but the way he looked at you gave me tingles. Come to think of it, this is the best news ever. Hot guy, son of super nice boss, wants to engage in coital bliss with you. We should be celebrating with wine." Sierra, who barely constrained herself, held two thumbs up.

Ariel smiled at the symbol of approval. "Yeah, I see your point."

"Where is he now?" Sierra asked pursing her lips in an attempt to look serious.

"I left him aroused under the oak tree looking rather perplexed. Here's the thing. I received a call from the Naval hospital on my way here and the doctors have taken my brother out of the induced coma. He's awake, and apparently cracking jokes."

"Oh, my. Sounds like John. What's the prognosis?"

"I'll see him tomorrow and evaluate the current situation for myself. There will be a series of in-house treatments but once they're over and I verify his release date, I'm relocating him home to the farm." Bracing her hands on her hips, she continued, "I have responsibilities, Sierra, and no time for romance or any kind of involvement complication." She bit her knuckles. "But it was the hottest almost sex I've ever had. I've never been so consumed, so desired and half-taken before. I keep replaying it in my mind and I get, you know…physical sensations. There was a definite connection, like we fit together."

"Ariel, listen to me. You've been through so much with 'he who won't be named' ex-boyfriend, your mother's death, overseeing care for John since his injury…the list goes on, girlfriend. My advice to you is grab the moment by the…never mind. Enjoy this adventure and no regrets. What does Gavin do for a living?"

Ariel's shoulders raised and lowered as she let out a heavy sigh, "He's in the military. He's a Special Forces military guy and a frickin' SEAL, right at the top of my do not get involved with list."

Sierra couldn't hide her surprise. "I'm speechless. Honest. No words."

"Well, there's a first." Ariel chuckled into her bottle of water.

"Hey, no fair," Sierra objected, punching Ariel's exposed thigh before she continued. "You'd rather go dumpster diving than have anything to do with a military guy. I guess it wouldn't help to point out he's not a Marine like your Dad and brother and therefore not first on the front lines of combat. I know what they do is also dangerous but isn't it more covert, like under the cover of darkness sneak in and sneak out type of operations?" She walked her fingers stealthily across the bar top.

Ariel groaned in response. "He calls his dog a hair missile, for Pete's sake and he is Jeff's son. You don't think he'll tell Jeff we were grinding on each other under the oak tree, do you?"

"Are you kidding?" Sierra leaned forward to emphasize her sincerity. "Those guys wrote the book on how to keep a secret. Trust me, a tough Navy SEAL would not run to his Daddy. Besides, Jeff is perceptive enough to observe what is going on between you two, all on his own."

Ariel frowned, contemplative.

"Is there something else?" Sierra asked, while filling her over-sized cup with fresh-brewed coffee.

Ariel nodded. "Last night when Gavin bumped into Drake keying my truck at our favorite watering hole."

Sierra raised her eyebrows. "Would you call Gavin bloodying Drake's nose being bumped into?"

"Okay. Not exactly, but a connection registered with Gavin when the dumbass keyed my truck. It's obvious Gavin has questions about our possible link but I'm not ready to rehash my past with him or anyone. It's over and it stays over." Ariel clenched her fists in her lap.

"Sorry girlfriend." Sierra clasped Ariel's shoulders. "Drake reignited the past last night. I vote for telling Mr. SEAL the truth. It's not your fault Drake is such a dick. Besides, this Gavin guy deals with terrorists and other unsavory characters on a daily basis. He'll dial in on this, I promise. What did you say when you left him all alone by your couple's tree?"

"Not a thing, Miss Smart-ass. I saluted him and took off in my truck."

"Okay. You definitely need to go back and talk to him, like now. I mean, if you ever want to have full on, all the way sex with him. And you do want to ride his particular train, don't you?"

Ariel clenched and unclenched her fists. "What I'd like to do and what I need to do are two entirely different things. Besides, I saluted and left after a mutual groping session for God's sake, so I can't simply breeze back over to chat it up with him."

Sierra let go of Ariel's shoulders and waved her arms in a get going move. "Sure you can."

Encouraged by her friend's straightforward advice, Ariel admitted, "I'm embarrassed but you're right. I'll take care of it."

"Whatever you need R. I'm here for you." Sierra's emerald eyes flashed apparent concern.

Ariel picked up her purse from the back of the stool, slung it over her shoulder, and stood to go. "You're the best, Sierra. This talk has helped me face the much more important situation of seeing John tomorrow. I better head out."

They strolled arm-in-arm to the front door and warmly hugged goodbye. Ariel faced her oldest and dearest friend. "I most definitely want to ride the sexy SEAL train," she said with an impish wink and shut the door behind her.

Chapter 7

Gavin Cross didn't consider himself a ladies man but women usually ran toward him and not away from him, especially after a mind-blowing make-out session like today. Ariel had made a huge impact on him. She'd really gotten under his skin, like no other, not even his passion for the Teams. And worse, he never visualized himself as a man who would allow himself the luxury of passionate emotion.

There was no doubt in his mind he had serious hots for Dr. Armstrong. And what was with the disappearing act? She was adept at the maneuver as she'd demonstrated more than once. Maybe his intensity scared her off. He'd been accused of being intense more than once. The nickname, Caveman, was born out of his brazen attempts at picking up women in bars. His lines were simple, "You want to dance?" Then, "You want to go home with me?" As a SEAL he liked the direct approach. What was he supposed to do? Ask, "What's your sign?" Besides, this Navy guy wasn't looking for a long-term gig. He promised himself he'd avoid creating any widows while he played war. During his time as a SEAL, he'd attended more than one funeral of a teammate downed by an enemy's bullet. He'd witnessed the grieving widow's endless tears and the bewildered look on the fatherless children's faces. Nope. It was too much to ask of anyone truly loved to endure the hardship of untimely death.

Gavin shoved off the oak he'd been leaning against. The morning was slipping away which meant chores waited. He grabbed his gun bag and headed back to his jeep. He realized he'd have to play it cool with the Doctor if he wanted his questions answered. Gavin needed to become Mr. Chill. He laughed at the idea. Stand down Petty Officer Cross. You are such an angry asshole. Being a SEAL was all about control and discipline. It was also about not backing down in a difficult situation but manning up and getting the job done. He missed being in the action. He lived for the camaraderie with the team guys. The past months in a god-forsaken land away from family, friends, and beer, tested even the strongest of wills. No doubt, it had tested his strength to the max.

He resolved to get to the bottom of the Dr. Armstrong dog tag mystery before he headed back to his team. Gavin jumped in his jeep and whipped it around toward home.

Defensive urban driving, one of the many courses Gavin took as part of his extensive training, was high on his favorite's list. Right now, he was content to bounce along on the pot-holed dirt road using his knee as his rudder. Keeping it real, he mused. His thoughts drifted back to the carnal pleasure which had left him speechless and horny under the oak tree this morning as the jeep continued vibrating across the ruts. His gut knotted in a familiar reaction he hadn't experienced since high school and his first crush.

The sun's shimmer reflected off the barn's tin roof as he rounded the corner of the tree line. Gavin flipped down the sun visor and stepped on the brake before crossing the metal cattle guard into the main yard. Was she here, working? He wondered. The grass lot where everyone parked behind the barn was empty. Gavin shifted into neutral and cut the ignition so the car rolled the final distance into his parking space. He stepped out, stretched his neck to the right and left, checking for signs of activity. No one was around. Probably better she wasn't here. Yeah, right. He growled to himself. The way she tore out of the pasture she had somewhere to be and maybe someone to meet.

Determined to clear his mind he grabbed a nearby pitchfork and headed into the barn. He mucked stalls until sweat soaked his shirt and the clench in his gut released. Time for a beer. With his arms stretched over his head, he walked out of the barn and squinted at the blazing Florida sun starting its descent toward the horizon. The prospect of an ice-cold brewsky coating his parched throat made his mouth water. He opened the screen door and stepped into the kitchen. "Make it a cold one, bar keep," he called out as he opened the refrigerator door and grabbed a Corona.

****

Later, Gavin placed the empty beer bottle on the counter and meandered out to the front yard as the night sky filled with infinite stars and a crescent moon; he took advantage of the unobstructed view life in the country offered. He glanced in the direction of the guest cottage and noticed no lights shone from the windows but Ariel's truck was parked out front. It was time for answers. He turned toward the path leading straight to her front porch. Wait, no way Mr. Chill would storm the cottage, he realized, and abruptly changed course back to the ranch house.

Chapter 8

The trip to Jacksonville was a welcomed relief from the unexpected excitement of the day before. A hot summer breeze whipped through the windows of the doctor's truck and massaged her sun-kissed face. She merged onto the highway, turned on the air conditioner, and raised the windows. Glancing briefly down, she punched the channel button for country music. One of her favorites sang on the radio. As she tapped the steering wheel keeping time to the rhythmic tempo, her shoulders relaxed and a warm feeling of contentment replaced the anxiety tensing her back muscles. The song ended and her mind immediately wandered into reviewing the events of yesterday one more time, including the 'almost' sex. Well, if she was honest with herself, mostly the 'almost' sex. She tingled as she remembered Gavin running his large weathered hand up and down her back and pausing as he caressed her bottom. A drop of sweat rolled down her cheek and her face flushed. She'd have to prevent another close encounter from happening, no matter how good his tongue felt invading her mouth while his hands stroked her eager body.

Aside from her own hard and fast rule to never date military men, she was curious about his sudden appearance on the farm which might require another face to face. Yeah, she had her own set of questions for

Mr. Danger. In spite of his controlled outward demeanor, his trigger was cocked. The minute he appeared from behind the tree in the pasture she sensed his "king of everything" confidence, ready to end any intrusion on his territory. For a second she could have sworn he was looking at an enemy combatant and not her. She'd witnessed the same intensity in a stallion passing the stall of another intact male. It was nothing to take lightly so she'd make sure she didn't let her guard down again.

Traffic buzzed by as she slowed down to make the turn off Jacksonville's 295 beltway , to the Highway 15 exit. Traveling North to Birmingham Street she turned right and rolled slowly down Child Street until she spied the giant white monolithic building on the left. The Naval Hospital Jacksonville sprawled out in front of her. The pit of her stomach tightened at the prospect of seeing her beloved younger brother. His injuries were catastrophic and most probably permanent. But he was alive and so, so lucky. Fortunately, there were Spec Ops nearby who radioed for an evac helicopter and airlifted him to a Combat Army Support Hospital at Bagram Air Base pronto or he would be dead and she wouldn't be making this trip. Bile rose up in her throat as she recalled receiving news of John's injury. Her subsequent conversations with Captain Jack Stern, who let it slip there had been a SEAL team assigned to protect and provide cover for her brother's unit, kept her temper at a boil. She held the SEALs responsible for the accident. Where were their snipers when the Taliban planted an IED? Why hadn't they scouted the area? What about their bomb-sniffing dogs? All questions begged to be answered but in good time. The number one priority was getting John ready for life at home. She had already decided not to discuss the accident unless he mentioned it first. Her immediate task was finding out his specific program for recovery and how much was possible. She needed to know what to expect and be prepared to see him for the first time since he'd come out of his coma. She had wanted to come earlier but Captain Jack had convinced her to wait.

Ariel maneuvered her truck into the first available parking space and peered up at the many windows of the hospital wondering if John could see her. She gathered her notebook and scowled as she stepped out of her truck into the blistering Florida heat, the humid air so thick it approximated a sauna. Clutching a crumpled piece of paper with John's room number on it, she headed for the first set of glass doors and air conditioning. Ariel checked her watch and found she was early, as usual, so she veered left toward the coffee kiosk directly inside the building.

"What can I get for you, ma'am?" the barista asked as he wiped his hands on his checkered apron.

"I'd like a grande latte with one raw sugar, and a hot chocolate with whipped cream, no lid," she said as she took a twenty-dollar bill from her billfold. *God, for a tough guy, John turned kid where his hot chocolate, 'hold the lid which mushed his whipped cream too far into the hot beverage,' was concerned.* She remembered their many Saturday trips to the local coffee cafe together when he could barely see the top of the counter and recalled exactly how he liked his drink. She smiled, lifted the carrier with two drinks, and headed for the elevators.

The long sterile hallway past the nurse's station to room 404 reminded Ariel of her satisfaction with the choice to be a veterinarian and not a medical doctor. As a horse lover, she much preferred the aroma of fresh mowed hay to the smell of overfilled bedpans. She skirted past bandaged young men in wheel chairs with IV lines trailing beside them. One of them winked at her. She touched his arm and grinned back. He was probably somebody's brother and definitely someone's son. At least, he made it back. These broken pieces in the game of war were the fortunate ones. Her father had not been so lucky.

"Are you Ariel Armstrong?" A deep masculine voice bounced her back to the present. She nodded yes and looked up to see a handsome thirty something man in scrubs.

She stuck out her hand to shake his and asked, "And you are?"

"Dr. Remington Lewis but most people call me Remmy," he hesitated, glancing quickly down at her name tag again. "You're a doctor?"

Ariel laughed, placing her hand on her visitor's badge. "Oh, force of habit from daily signing my name on scripts, lab reports and, well, I'm a veterinarian, not a medical doctor."

He smiled, accentuating the dimple dividing the middle of his chin. "Same amount of time in school and I have an advantage which makes my job easier than yours. My patients can tell me what's wrong. So, we're on a first name basis, Ariel."

God, he's a beautiful man with bedside manners out the wazoo but let's see how much medicine he knows. Ariel followed the hunky doctor into John's room taking in the condition of her younger brother as he lay in bed, eyes closed. His neck was still in a brace and obvious cuts and scratches on his arms and face from the accident but nothing deep enough to leave an ugly scar. The damage, per what Casualty Assistance Officer, Jack Stern had told her, was from the chest down.

Her heart ached as she observed her brother's sleepy eyes open and lock on her, a smile spreading quickly across his chapped, split lips.

"Hey Sis, about time you dragged your butt in here to see me." He beamed. "I see you met my Doc. And it looks like you brought me something from the café downstairs. Would it be my favorite hot chocolate with whipped cream?"

Ariel corralled her brother in a tight hug, unwilling to let go, "Correct, cowboy. How's it going?" She held the drink up as if it were a trophy and touched it to her lips for a temperature test before tilting the cup's edge to her brother's lips, allowing him access to the protruding straw."

"A little worse for wear so they say, hey Doc?" John replied, tilting his chin toward the doctor. "Oh man. Good hot chocolate," he grinned at his sister, licking the whipped cream off his lips.

The doctor replied with a deadpan smile, "Let's have a look." He placed the stethoscope on John's chest and shifted the flat metal end from side to side while he listened intently with his ear buds. "Strong heart," he replied, a pinched half-smile on his lips.

"Pure heart," Ariel added, touching her brother's shoulder.

The doctor wrapped the instrument around his neck

and probed John's arms and hands, nodding in affirmative as he progressed down the body. He glanced in Ariel's direction and gently peeled back the covers from John's waist, revealing two motionless legs.

She met his gaze and suppressed a gasp as she came to grasp with the reality of her brother's lifeless limbs.

Dr. Lewis continued in a matter-of-fact manner poking and pinching John's legs, as he noted any reflex or lack of one, each time looking expectantly at his patient. "Can you feel this?"

The ache in Ariel's heart expanded at each pronouncement of "no, nothing," and she realized she'd been holding her breath, waiting for one tiny, little, "yes." Suddenly, the extreme nature of her brother's injuries hit her and her knees buckled. The room started a slow spin. She clutched the bed frame, determined not to allow the tsunami of fear and grief to overtake her.

Remington suddenly but artfully ended the exam and smoothed the covers over his patient. She wondered if he sensed her imminent meltdown. He motioned for her to follow him into the hall. Giving her brother's leg a final squeeze, he addressed his patient, "Be back in a minute, John."

Ariel wobbled out of the room and weaved her way behind the doctor down the hall into a well-appointed office, decorated with unusual military memorabilia like a hand-grenade paperweight and artillery shell bookends. The transformation in Remington's expression from the poker-faced doctor to somber physician aroused her suspicions. She dreaded the next few minutes. But no matter what news he laid on her, she'd be there for her brother. And no matter the outcome, John would soldier-on in the Armstrong family tradition. They'd face the hardship side by side.

Ariel braced herself. "Give it to me straight, Doctor Lewis."

Motioning her to take a seat, he reluctantly conveyed his prognosis. "First of all, imparting news of this nature is the aspect of being a doctor I dislike the most. I'm sure receiving the prognosis is tougher." He paused, as if choosing his words. "You already know John suffered catastrophic injuries in his accident. He has three broken vertebrae, two of which we fused in surgery and the third will hopefully fuse on its own. Your brother will most likely be in a wheel chair for the rest of his life. He's currently a paraplegic." He tightened his grip on the arms of the chair. His eyes filled with compassion. "But it's not all dire news. There's no brain damage or internal injury and he's a fighter. Attitude is a major factor in treatment of these kinds of traumas. I recommend we start physical therapy right away. We'll advance him as far as he can go. I estimate he'll break all the limits."

An errant tear rolled down her cheek and she swiped it away. Her chest heaved. "This is worse than I expected." The words tumbled out, "I don't want his hopes built up he'll walk again if there's no chance. He needs to be told his military career is over. Someone has to tell him he'll never resume scout patrol with his Marine buddies." She grimaced and slowly shook her head. "He's going to be pissed, so pissed. I think the anger will consume him."

Remington stabbed his finger in his own chest. "Look at me, Ariel. He's alive. His reflexes indicate good mobility in his hands and arms. He is capable of living a full and rewarding life, so let's keep the faith. Your attitude as care giver is essential."

Ariel glanced in the direction of her brother's room. "You're right. Whatever he needs, Doctor. What's our first action?" She exhaled and sat up straight, waiting for his answer.

He nodded. "I recommend water therapy. We'll get him started at the pool here. Once he's home you can drive him back for treatment or we can have a physical therapist come to you. There are also numerous exercises geared to strengthen his legs to keep them from atrophying. We'll set him up in a non-motorized wheel chair so he has to use his arms to get around."

"When will he be ready to come home?" she asked glancing around the office at the walls filled with awards and commendations. They were all inscribed with the name Remington Lewis.

"In a few weeks, maybe a month." He rose from the chair and stepped closer to Ariel. "Listen, I know this is tough but I'm here with you every step of the way."

Her eyes burned. Her shoulders shook. "It's so overwhelming to see him like this knowing it's his future. Doc, he was a champion swimmer in college, a superb athlete."

He helped her out of the chair and squeezed both her arms. "There're a number of support groups I can refer you to, but bottom line, I'm here for the duration of his treatments, Ariel." His obvious warmth and sincerity endeared him to her but she couldn't respond. Emotionally drained and mentally frozen, she stood there in his embrace for what seemed like hours.

Remington gently released Ariel and in a soft tone, asked, "You okay?"

She nodded. "Exhausted, but I'll be okay."

"Go wash up and meet me back in John's room. I need to go over his prognosis with him and I think it'd be important to have you present." He handed her a tissue.

"I want to be there," she sniffled. "Give me a few minutes." She blew her nose and straightened her blouse.

"No problem. I'll arrange his therapy schedule with him while we wait." He turned to leave.

"I appreciate everything you're doing for John," Ariel called out. "He's in good, no great hands."

"Same goes for you, Doctor," he replied before he vanished down the hall.

Surveying the plethora of commendations and framed medical merits surrounding her, she muttered to herself, "It's going to be a long haul but I can't think of anyone I'd rather have watching my back or John's than you, Dr. Remington Lewis."

Chapter 9

The darkness helped her think. Concentrate. Focus. It had been a hell of a day but rocking on the front porch, incognito between two giant planted palms, settled her mind. Sipping Merlot only added to the evening's perfection. A westerly breeze tempered the humid night air and the stars, unhampered by a city glow, winked at her in a spontaneous dance. Her body melted in relaxation.

Ariel secretly spied on Gavin as he exited the barn and veered toward his family home. *What were his real intentions toward her? Was he hoping to score round two?* She exhaled a deep sigh when he swung open the screen door and disappeared into the main house. She wasn't ready to add any more 'busy' to the day. Ariel took another sip of room temperature wine. She savored the red liquid on her lips and swished it over her tongue before swallowing. Her favorite wine glided down her throat and spread in a warm burst into her stomach. At least, she assigned the wine with making her stomach feel warm all over. She couldn't let him get to her. There was too much at stake. Ariel focused her attention on John lying in his hospital bed, remembering how brave he acted. It made her even more resolute to get him to the farm as soon as possible. Hospitals were dreary places for the unfortunate. Maybe Dr. Lewis would make house calls to check on

John's progress so her brother wouldn't have to endure the monthly haul for checkups. She could certainly think of a lot worse things than beholding the oh-so-fine doctor for an hour. Even better, he'd probably suit up in a pair of swim trunks for the water therapy in the family's Florida necessity swimming pool. *My flavor of stress relief.* She smiled. *Good time to crack open my new romance novel. I'll sleep better after a few hours of reading about someone else's relationship drama.*

****

Ariel strained against the heaviness of her eyelids and forced her eyes open. She yawned and stretched her arms over her head. Checking her watch, the hands rested at eleven. "Time to get ready for some much needed sleep," she said between a yawn, leaning forward to stand up after one last rock back and forth. Glass in hand she headed for the kitchen to set her morning coffee. She'd be hitting the start button way too soon from now.

The curtains in the kitchen hung half way open. As she stood on tiptoes to close them, a figure crossed in front of the light from an upstairs window of the main house and caught her eye. She squinted past the night shadows and peered into the dimly lit room across the courtyard. The male figure silhouetted in the window slipped by in a crouched position, arms extended. *What the hell?* Arms balanced on the kitchen sink, Ariel leaned forward. *Good god, is he holding a gun in his hand? Are they being robbed? Or worse?*

Ariel was aware both Jeff and Gavin were armed and capable of defending themselves, but what if the intruder surprised them. *What if they got into a gunfight while she stood peering out of her window? She had to act.* She raced to her room and retrieved her own pistol stored in her night stand, and stayed low to the ground in case he could see her as well. She racked the 9mm barrel back, chambered a bullet, and flipped off the safety, making sure to carry out the sequence as quietly as possible in case he had an accomplice. Sound carried out here in the country and she needed to locate the intruder or intruders. Ariel closed her eyes, relying solely on sound, and listened. Silence. All the firearms training in the world was useless at a time like this unless she stayed calm and focused. Her brother had drilled similar scenarios into her over and over, and taught her self-defense before he deployed six months ago. John had asserted ensuring her safety was his mission and he'd been a relentless instructor.

Ariel settled her nerves and headed for the back door grabbing her cell phone off the kitchen counter. She checked to make sure the sound was turned off and stuffed it in her back pocket. Confident in her shooting skills, she decided to survey the situation first before calling the Sheriff and stepped forward, gripping the pistol in both hands. Besides, by the time law enforcement arrived way out here, everyone could be dead.

With the kitchen doorjamb as cover, she peered around the corner and almost dropped her gun. Gavin, Wager slinking at his side, maneuvered along the driveway dressed in the light brown camouflage the military uses for combat in deserts, like Afghanistan. His night vision goggles perched on his face like an alien mask. Half crouching but with the agility of an Olympic athlete, he rotated his pistol right to left as if ready for an ambush. No doubt about it, he was on patrol.

"No way," she murmured to herself. Her chest tightened. She swallowed to relieve the sudden dryness captured in her throat preventing words from coming out. Gavin lurked around outside with a gun? She needed to get closer to make sense out of the crazy scene unfolding before her. The downside to the plan was Gavin's potential state of mind. What or maybe whom was he hunting? There were also Wager's keen animal perceptions to consider. If her actions alerted his attention to her the results could be deadly. But what if she directed the canine's attention away from her? If Gavin unloaded his weapon in the direction of Wager's bark, it would give her time to intervene.

Ariel peeked around the corner of the door so fast, the rush of air brushed her hair back, as she jumped behind the safety of the door. Gavin, with Wager glued to his side, crept along the side of her small frame house. She detected his lips moving but the words were slurred as if he was mumbling out loud. No Spec Ops action she'd ever read about involved talking while pursuing an enemy. Not an expert herself, she relied on her brother who loved regaling her with his live-action war stories. His renditions emphasized hand signals, rather than verbiage, used between the men to operate. The only explanation she could fathom for the bizarre behavior was...nothing. She had absolutely nothing. She had no clue why Gavin would be out patrolling his own property in battle gear.

The only way to resolve this mystery was direct confrontation. Ariel slipped the pistol's safety lever to the on position and tucked it securely in her back waistband. She leaned forward to crack open her screen door. As her hand gripped the handle, Gavin muttered, as if speaking into a headpiece, "Bravo this is Caveman. Outpost is secure." He lowered and holstered his gun, raised his night vision goggles to his forehead and veered left in the direction of his front door. Ariel observed, dumbfounded, as the badass Navy SEAL disappeared into the house, Wager at his heels.

Holy Crap. What just happened? Ariel clutched her pounding chest as she slipped back into the shadows of her darkened kitchen. Her breath caught in jagged intakes and her neck muscles twitched as she struggled to grasp the surreal scene, well, more like an episode, she'd just witnessed. She treated horses with heightened agitation every time she stuck a hypodermic needle into their neck. Dogs suffering from separation anxiety were nothing new. She could totally deal with four legged dilemmas but what puzzled her most was Gavin, a man who seemed completely in control. He certainly showed commendable restraint earlier today in the pasture, under the oak tree. Something is obviously going on with him, but what?

"Wager," she mused out loud. He displayed a telling clue with his clinginess during the episode. He looked stressed and almost feral when she reviewed his behavior. The sudden tail wagging as they scrambled up the front porch stairs to the house was a noteworthy change. Hummm. Was Wager signaling, "Mission accomplished? Now be my best buddy again?"

She couldn't comprehend a reason for his bizarre behavior other than sleepwalking. The realization hit her like someone plowed a fist into her chest. A lethally dangerous man was sleepwalking with a loaded gun. She tried to calm her breathing but could only inhale tiny gasps of air while her head buzzed with the dilemma of what to do. Should she tell Jeff or call the sheriff and have him sort it out with Gavin? Maybe Remington would know what to do because she sure as hell didn't. One thing was certain; she needed to get some sleep. There was no substitute for a cool head and clear thinking when handling a hot mess of a situation like this one.

Chapter 10

Ariel collapsed in her desk chair and took a furtive sip from the steaming cup of fresh brewed coffee. Weary from a long night of tossing and turning, she fired up her computer noting the early morning fog out her window as she waited for the browser home page to appear. *Mr. Google, you're going to be my best friend today.* She briskly tapped the keys, spelled out, 'sleep-walking' and waited, as lines of titles about sleep-walking rolled down the screen thinking, *searching the internet...my new contact sport. Hummm, no lack of information on this subject but where to start? More importantly, what data is true?*

Here's one from the Veterans Administration. She clicked on the link. The site opened and the letters PTSD jumped out in bold red. She held her breath and clicked again. Ariel's world tipped on its axis as she recited the words out loud, "Post Traumatic Stress Disorder." Certainly aware of PTSD, she'd never in her wildest dreams considered she'd ever experience it first-hand. Scanning the page, she continued, consumed by the seriousness of the information scrolling down the screen. She verbally ticked off the symptoms, "sleep walking, check, aversion to loud noises, no check, anger issues, pounding on my ex in a parking lot suggests a probable check, uncontrollable crying, a big no check, physically active nightmares, based on last night, check."

The warning signs continued but Ariel hit the red X in the upper right hand corner of the window and closed the document. She'd read enough to know her life just became more complicated. The real problem was what to do about her discovery. She needed to clear her head. More urgently, she must guard her heart.

The doctor mentally scanned the day's schedule. Pre-purchase examinations were required on a few horses Jeff had shown interest in buying so she slipped on a fresh smock, her unofficial uniform, required when she represented the farm off site. She also needed to perform one on a cute two-month-old burro he wanted for a barn companion and smiled at the memory of him braying so hard his body shook the first time she visited him. *Yeah, she'd call on the burro farm first.*

Ariel slid on her jeans. She grabbed her work boots and balanced first on one foot, then the other as she tugged the leather over well-worn socks. Ready for work, she bolted out the door and ran head on into a human brick wall...Jeff.

"Dr. Armstrong, where's the fire?"

Surprised by the one person she wanted to avoid this morning, she peeled herself off his chest, "Nowhere, I mean nowhere around here." Scarlet-colored heat ascended her face. *A quick count to five ought to do it. One, two, three...full composure.* "I'm heading out to Winding Creek farms to check out Garcia."

A puzzled look crossed his face as Jeff scratched his head, "Who's Garcia?"

"Garcia is the spanking cute baby burro you're considering as a barn companion for Nike." She grinned like a loon and hoped her over-the-top bubbly tone would keep the subject of Gavin off the table until she figured out the best way to approach Jeff with her revelation.

"Ah," his face lit up, "I like the name. He's the exact reason I showed up at your front door. If you complete the pre-purchase exam and determine Garcia's the right temperament for Nike, which is a nice way of saying he's so calm he's almost comatose," he chuckled, "go ahead and trailer him home. I've made arrangements with his owner for payment." Jeff dangled truck keys in his right hand. "Here, drive my truck. Gavin's hitching up the trailer."

Oh damn. The mention of his name acted like a trigger and a torrent of confusion washed over her. She was swimming, no, flailing in uncharted waters. *Should she share what she witnessed now and risk causing Jeff another heart attack? Maybe talking to Gavin, as intimidating as it seemed, was the best course.* The haunting images of last night engulfed her. *Did Jeff know about his son's, she wasn't sure what to call it, 'condition?' If so, why hadn't he warned her?*

The space on the front porch suddenly condensed. Cornered with no escape, she gulped for air but couldn't seem to breathe enough into her aching lungs. Sweat trickled down the sides of her scalp as she wrung her clammy palms. Was the front porch spinning? Her vision blacked out as she crumpled in a heap onto the redwood deck.

"Ariel." Her name sounded as if it was being called from somewhere in the distance. The taste of cold water wetted her lips. She smacked them together savoring the clean, fresh taste. A hand rested on her forehead and another one held her wrist, taking her pulse she guessed. The voice called closer, "Ariel, are you okay?" She blinked her eyes open and found herself propped up on a well-built, hairy chest. With a pretended air of nonchalance, she fumbled for the closest support to help her stand and grabbed a handful of substantial thigh muscle.

"Sure, yeah, I'm okay, just got a little dizzy." *God, the spinning is disorienting.* She blinked again, attempting to shake off the muddle in her brain as she grabbed the hand extended to help her up. Jeff, relief on his face and concern clouding his eyes, visually followed her motion until she steadied herself.

He lowered his voice to a whisper, "You had us worried, Doctor."

Ariel opened her mouth to answer and snapped her lips shut. *Wait a minute. Us?* She jerked her head around as Gavin, bare-chested in camouflage pants, gracefully leapt to his feet hovering beside her with equal attention. She stared at the male perfection next to her, taking in his half-naked, suntanned body. With a perfect design of fine, dark chest hair curved down into a thin, straight line she understood the reference to 'happy trail' and was damn sure this one led to all kinds of joy. She turned her attention back to Jeff, determined not to indulge her fantasy.

"Fortunately, Gavin was close by and knows first aid." Jeff still sounded a bit distraught.

"I'm so sorry to worry you both, but I'm fine. I didn't get much sleep last night and then I skipped breakfast this morning, a recipe for low blood sugar and well, fainting, I guess." Ariel apologized, embarrassed, she slid her hands in her rear pockets and rocked back on her heels.

"I'd better get going to Winding Creek before the day gets away from me." She stooped for the keys she dropped earlier, surreptitiously wiping the beads of nervous sweat off her top lip.

"Hang on Ariel. I don't think it's such a good idea to go driving all over the countryside after a fall. Gavin can chauffeur you today."

She peeked at the undeniably handsome son of her boss SEAL and yep, he was piercing her with a shit-eating grin, accentuating the dimple in his chin. He folded his muscular arms across his massive chest, closely observing her, no doubt waiting to see how she would try to squirm out of the arrangement. *Screw it. Time to get some questions answered.*

"Well, if it's okay with Gavin," she challenged, mocking him and folding her arms across her chest. "But shouldn't you finish getting dressed?" She flicked her finger at his half-naked body.

Gavin scooped up the keys, placed his hand in the small of Ariel's back, and nudged her forward. "Wait here, smarty pants. I'll get the trailer and be right back," he riposted.

Jeff arched his eyebrow and directed a questioning glance to Ariel. "Are you sure you feel up for this? We can postpone the purchase if you want to stay here and rest."

Ariel stepped off the porch as she signaled to Jeff the all's okay sign with her thumb up. Gavin exited the truck and without missing a beat, repositioned his hand firmly on Ariel's back. With a wink to his father he spoke to Ariel, "Ma'am. Let's hit it and get it. Daylight's burning."

****

She didn't quite know how to breach the quiet as she studied the broken white lines on the highway out the windshield. Gavin drove in silence, his face unreadable. *Does he have any idea what he did last night? He's wearing the same camo pants. Did he sleep in them? If so, he'd surely register something was off, wouldn't he? Other than his brooding muteness, nothing seemed out of the ordinary with him. But then, what was he supposed to say after I left him standing under the oak tree, breathing hard. Don't go there, Ariel or you'll be panting like a dog in a hundred degree heat.* She glanced over at him, one arm on the window ledge, one arm extended to the top of the steering wheel. He was staring straight ahead like he didn't have a care in the world.

The sound of a phone ringing startled her out of her musings. She grabbed her cell out of its holder on her waist and answered, "Dr. Armstrong."

She spoke in chopped communication, "Um, yes, sounds good. I can do that. Maybe later tonight? Bye." She shoved the phone back in the belt case and punched the on button for the radio.

"Who was on the phone?" Gavin asked, trying to sound casual.

"Oh, a client inquiring about medication he needs." Ariel responded equally as earnest to sound nonchalant.

With a noticeable edge to his voice Gavin questioned her, "Yeah, so you deliver medication at night to male clients? What are you, the midnight medicine express?"

"What? No, I mean not usually. He has a sick horse...wait a minute. I don't have to explain myself to

89

you." Her voice rose in indignation.

"Damn straight, you don't," Gavin shouted. "You can stay out all night long with whomever you want, doing whatever you want and then faint from lack of sleep but I won't be your dumb-ass driver again."

"You are a dumb-ass if you think I was out all night with a guy. Actually, the truth is I *was* out all night with a guy," she intentionally paused to observe his reaction, "you." She spit the final word out, exasperated.

"What?" His face twisted in confusion. He glanced across the front seat, as if mapping every inch of her face.

Ariel sensed he was searching his brain for an answer as his eyes zipped from side to side like a pinball, trying to spit an answer out the chute. *He doesn't have a clue*. As she weighed her options, compassion blossomed inside her. Do I tell him? How do I tell him? I haven't even done the fundamental research to comprehend what I'm babbling about. She swallowed hard. He has to know.

She fidgeted with her hands as she started, "You and Wager, last night, were walking, no you were patrolling out in front of my cottage. Do you remember being out late in the evening?" She consciously delivered the question without incrimination.

He caught the accusation and tromped on it. "Patrolling? Are you serious? You must have been dreaming, sweetheart," he punched out the last word.

Ariel's stomach clenched as the air between them thickened. She cringed in fear, raising her arms to protect her face from the slap previous experience dictated would come next. The dog tags dangled between her breasts while she tenuously edged her way across the seat as far away from him as she could get. She clutched the door handle ready to jump out. She'd been down this path before. She'd become expert at predicting the outcome of an angry encounter with the opposite sex. Her pulse quickened. At the next intersection red light she'd leap. She steadied her breathing, and focused her mind on reading the road signs ahead. Gavin's foot lifted off the accelerator and time slowed as the truck rolled to a stop. Ariel yanked the handle, hard. Nothing. She used her shoulder and rammed the doorframe while her opposite hand tugged on the lever. Someone grabbed her from behind. She turned and swung her fist, making contact with a cement jaw line.

"Holy crap," she howled. Recoiled by the acute ache in her knuckles, Ariel ended her escape attempts and gingerly rubbed the top of her hand. Click. The sound of the lock opening averted her attention to the window ledge. She turned to see the button on the door had popped up. Remorse seeped into every pore of her body as reality hit her. She turned to face Gavin.

"The door was locked to keep other people out, not keep you in," Gavin scrutinized every inch of her distraught face. "All you had to do was ask, Doctor Armstrong, and you'd be free to go."

She was sure it was a double entendre but decided, for once, to withhold the temptation to challenge his comment. Besides, calling her Doctor Armstrong didn't exactly signify a truce.

"I thought for a minute you were someone else," she responded, her voice barely above a whisper. She grabbed the dog tags, letting the weight of them rest in her palm, trying to hide her embarrassment.

"Who else?" he asked, his tone demanding.

"Someone from my past," she admitted.

"A dark past, I take it," he winced, rubbing his jaw.

"I'm so sorry, Gavin. I don't know what possessed me." Her lips trembled and hot tears filled her eyes. "When you grabbed my shoulder, I was afraid you were going to hit me. No, I don't mean you were going to hit me. I mean someone else was going to hit me. For a split second." She stuttered. Tears streamed down her face but she wiped them away.

Tenderly, he used his index finger to wipe away a drop of smeared mascara sticking on her cheek. "You're afraid of the douche bag I caught trying to key your truck, aren't you?" he asked, as if it suddenly dawned on him.

"Yes, Drake Porter's his name."

"And hitting women is his game," Gavin spat, shaking his head in disgust. "Listen, baby, you don't have to worry about an asshole like him ever hurting you again. Not while I'm around."

Her heart melted. His concern was real. She had no doubt he would carry out his vow to protect her. No way she'd put the onerous responsibility on him.

"I appreciate you wanting to look out for me, I do, but I can take care of myself."

His lips formed a devilish grin as he stroked his bruised jaw line. "I can see you can."

"We better get going or we'll be late to our appointment at Winding Creek Farm," she smiled at him. "Sorry again about hitting you." She held out her hand to shake.

Gavin lifted her delicate hand to his lips and kissed

each knuckle lightly, keeping his eyes locked on hers. "You can make it up to me," he offered.

She didn't withdraw. "How?"

"Go on a date with me tonight. I'm talking about a fine Italian restaurant, a little vino and gelato for dessert. What do you say, Doctor?"

The potential of a romantic evening with Gavin tempted her in a carnal way. He was intoxicating and daring. Ariel struggled to suppress her desire and squelch the fire in her belly. Who was she kidding? She wanted him. Lust unfurled between her thighs. She yearned to have his hands and lips explore her entire body over and over.

"Yes." She breathed out in a raspy voice, eyes closed in dreamy anticipation.

Yes, indeed. Gavin stomped on the accelerator and sped down the highway to check out a burro named Garcia.

Chapter 11

Gavin perceived a shift in his attitude, a definite energy he hadn't enjoyed in what seemed like ages, as he relaxed against the flagpole centered in the circular drive outside the barn. To be honest, he hadn't experienced this kind of happy enthusiasm since he was in college playing lacrosse, hanging with his best friend, Tony Franco. College was a carefree time. He let out a heavy sigh. From lacrosse captain he'd been transformed into a force-of-will warrior trained to hunt down and eliminate the enemy. He surveyed the view in front of him. The bucolic environment of Wildwood Farms was an ideal way to grow up but a lacrosse scholarship and the idea of adventure in a new location beckoned to him. In his third year of college, he met and was wooed by the Navy recruiter who convinced the all-star athlete he had what it took to become an elite Navy SEAL. After talking to Tony and finding out his friend had similar ambitions, they agreed to join immediately after college. Then an event changing the world happened, 9/11. They both rushed to sign on the dotted line.

After eight deployments to hellholes all over the globe, he was still alive but how alive? Ariel ignited a spark, setting off a bonfire in his gut. Her lean athletic body tantalized him. He experienced a whole gamut of emotion around her. Everything from carnal desire to intellectual interest stirred deep in his soul. No doubt about it, the woman awakened a part of his male psyche buried by one hundred-two degree desert heat, IEDs, and way too many camels. He wanted this date to be perfect. A chance to honestly get to know the person behind the professional degree and find out why she grips those dog tags like a security blanket enticed him. The habit confirmed quite a poker tell and by the end of the night this special operator would call her hand. But first he needed to face his father and have a man-to-man talk about Ariel's revelation. He apparently 'patrols' the grounds in the middle of the night.

Gavin shoved off the flagpole and strode toward the barn where his Dad would be gloating over his new acquisition, Garcia, probably feeding the four legged cutie carrots. As he approached the barn door his father's voice cooed baby talk to the burro.

"Hey, little man, you like being scratched behind the ears?" Jeff asked.

Gavin slipped his hands in the pockets of his cargo pants and stepped out of the sun's glare into the dark cavernous barn, waiting for his eyes to adjust. "Hey Dad, got a minute?"

Jeff looked at Gavin and nodded his affirmation still smiling from rubbing Garcia. "What's on your mind, son?"

Gavin nervously jangled the loose change in his pocket and decided the best way to broach the subject was to blurt it out in his usual no nonsense, Caveman fashion. "Doctor Armstrong informed me I patrolled the perimeter of the farm in combat dress last night, apparently asleep and with my gun out of the holster...Dad." His defiant tone echoed the same rebellious emotion he displayed as the boy who attended lacrosse practice in lieu of completing farm chores. Yep. And from the stern frown clouding his father's face, recalcitrant son summed up what his Dad must be thinking.

Jeff stepped forward and wrapped his arm around Gavin's shoulder. "It was inevitable we'd need to have this conversation, son." He squeezed, hard. "Let's take a walk."

Gavin strode forward, in step with the senior Cross, his thoughts blurred. "You aren't surprised by my revelation?" *What the hell? Am I the last to know I'm fucked up?*

"Surprised? No, son. Concerned, yes."

Gavin continued walking in glum silence remembering Tony's smiling send-off. His phony act smacked of deceit. He should have spotted Tony was in on the joke, the son-of-a-bitch. *I wasn't being sent home on family leave to help my Dad. I was off-loaded because I'm screwed up.* Anger simmered close to the surface, threatening to boil over. As they ambled around the edge of the pond to a wooden dock, Gavin attempted to mute his resentment. In brooding silence he gazed out over his favorite childhood haunt, stocked with bass and filled with carefree memories. Numb from the realization he'd been betrayed by those closest to him, he leaned down to pick up a stone, perfect for skimming across the pond's shimmering surface. He wound up his right arm and released the first stone, watching it skip and bounce across the glassy surface.

"Still got it, I see," Jeff broke the silence.

"Well, apparently, I've got something," Gavin responded, obviously irritated.

Jeff folded his arms across his chest. "I get you're upset, son. You were blindsided by the news."

"You think?" he replied, his face twisted in hard, dark angles, barely containing the ire smoldering beneath the surface.

"Son," Jeff said flatly, "the man standing in front of me is a warrior and I couldn't be prouder but bottom line, he's in trouble. No need to sugar-coat it."

"Sugar-coat what?" he asked, hurling another stone across the murky water.

"Gavin, you were sent home due to battle fatigue…"

"You were in on this? For god's sake Dad, why didn't you tell me?"

"You know Chief O'Malley is a friend of mine from my old Navy days. He called and swore me to secrecy." Jeff held up one finger to stop a second interruption, "It was to protect you, son. You did something which could have gotten you thrown out of the SEAL Teams and the Navy."

Gavin's quest to fill in the blanks propelled him full throttle into lobbing questions at his father. "What the hell did I do? How did Tony get involved? Did the approval process fire all the way up the chain of command?" He continued, his voice laced with sarcasm, "Who else is privy to Tony's well-hatched plot? Is my career over?" Feet apart, fists clenched at his sides, he glared at his father wrapped in self-denial.

Jeff dropped his shoulders and sighed, "Gavin, the reality is," he paused, "to be blunt, you were sleep walking and drew a gun on Tony. He's the one who reported it to the Chief, as well as other symptoms he witnessed, like sweating and agitation." Jeff punched the last words, as he raised his eyebrow in a, 'you get my drift,' look. He tilted his head toward his son obviously waiting for a response.

Gavin's world fell off its axis and exploded in front of his eyes. He'd seen the scars branded on the psyche of other vets but the idea battle stress would be the bullet to drop him never entered his warrior mentality. His shoulders slumped as the anguish of the problem he faced registered and seared his nerves. Tiredness overwhelmed his body. Clasping the sides of his head, he dropped to his knees. With his eyes focused on the ground, his mind raced to fill in the blanks. He uttered in disbelief, "I could have killed my best friend and not even known I pulled the trigger. I don't remember a thing except Tony. I believed him taking my gun was a prank."

"But you didn't, son. And I, for one, am convinced you would have snapped awake or aborted the shot, aware at some level of consciousness Tony wasn't the enemy."

"Either way Dad, I'm broken. No good to the Teams, no good to you and certainly no good to Dr. Armstrong."

The older man's attention locked onto the mention of his farm vet. "I see. So the good Doc is part of the equation now?" His brows arched in a question mark.

Gavin nodded. "Yeah, I asked her out on a date and she accepted. I don't want to discuss it right now. I should probably cancel due to the fact I might do something stupid."

"Oh, I think she could have any man acting stupid, without battle stress present. You should follow through with your plans. The night out would be a nice break and you certainly deserve a breather right now."

"Who else knows about my situation?"

"Just the CO, the Chief, Platoon Officer in Charge, Tony as the medical officer, apparently Ariel, and me." Jeff could see his son's embarrassment in asking. "Oh yeah, and the doctor at the The Naval Hospital Jacksonville you're supposed to see. I meant to talk to you about him. Dr. Romero is a former SEAL, who like Tony, was a corpsman. He transferred his experience toward medical school credits and a degree after he suffered injuries in combat and couldn't operate as a SEAL any longer. He specializes in PTSD and Traumatic Brain Injury diagnosis and treatment."

Gavin stood stunned at the revelation. Post Traumatic Stress Disorder? No way. Not in the cards for this badass. The SEAL credo did not allow for disorders of any kind and he wasn't going to see a shrink, if Dr. Romero was a psychiatrist, even if he had served on the SEAL Teams. Period. End of Story.

Rest, yes. Farm work to unwind from the intensity of war, yes, but screw the doctor and his psychobabble or doctor babble. It didn't matter. He didn't need it.

"No. I mean it Dad. Not going to happen." All the determination required to propel him through the toughest military training in the world blazed anew in his soul. Any reservations he had about his ability to function as a SEAL were cancelled. He would fight to the bitter end.

"It's part of the treatment program. It's required before you can be reinstated back into service." He paused. "Your career, the one you've sacrificed so much for, is on the line. It's the one point totally nonnegotiable. Gavin, try to see it from the military's point of view. They have a highly skilled, impeccably trained operator capable of carrying out nearly impossible missions who is off the reservation. Son, you might think you're in control right now, but you're not, and by God, you need to be. Quite frankly, I'm surprised by your complete refusal to acquiesce."

Gavin absorbed the words but didn't speak. Instead, he brushed past the one person whose advice he trusted the most, shaking his head in a defiant negative.

I am so screwed.

Chapter 12

Gavin hesitated, his finger trembling as he dangled it above the doorbell, and then jammed the tip into the button. He straightened the hated necktie around his neck, stepped back, and waited for the door to open. A small bouquet of three sunflowers hugged his chest as a, he wasn't sure what—peace offering, show of friendship, most probably an obvious flirtation. The only thing he did know for certain was he hated wearing these damn nooses. A bead of sweat popped up on his forehead. Then another drop rolled down the side of his face. *Get a grip, man. You've faced jihadists bent on your destruction. You can deal with*...the door swung open, "one stunning woman in a very short black dress," he enunciated each word out loud.

Ariel blushed. "Are those for me?" Indicating the flowers now loosely held upside down.

He offered them to her and answered with a definitive, "Yes."

"How sweet. Sunflowers are my favorite. Come in for a minute while I put them in water." She brushed her index finger over the center of the bouquet closing her eyes. "They are so soft," she noted over her shoulder, as she turned toward the kitchen.

Gavin's eyes locked on to the gentle sway of her hips accentuated by four-inch heels she wore like a lingerie model. Instead of the usual ponytail, jeans smeared with god knows what, and cowboy boots, the doctor transformed into a leggy, svelte beauty with thick wavy brown hair cascading down her back. *What am I getting myself into? This woman isn't some barfly eager to hop in the sack with a horny Navy puke for the night. No sir. She's the kind of woman who is seeking exactly what I can't offer her, a future. I should about face right now and zip out the nearest exit. Good Lord, what happened to the promise I made myself not to get involved while I'm on active duty? I refuse to make a widow...*

"Ready to go?" Ariel stared curiously at him. "You shaved off your beard. I like the look."

Gavin tucked his doubts safely away in a shadowy corner of his mind. "Thanks." He stroked the side of his face as if still adapting to the missing bristle. "I hope you're hungry, baby," he said, tugging her by the hand toward the door.

****

"Is this table okay?" Gavin asked pointing to the intimate table for two in front of them. "I asked for this far corner so we could talk and because I like to have my back to the wall. Old habits." He laughed.

Ariel nodded. "It's perfect. By the way, very foo-foo restaurant you picked, Mr. Cross. Who knew you had such gourmet taste." She poked him in the ribs with her index finger. "And I do understand about the gunfighter seat."

He ignored her finger prod and teasing. "You know about the gunfighter seat?"

"Yeah, my father was a Marine. My mother claimed he always reserved the seat with his back to the wall, no exceptions."

Gavin noticed sadness tinged her voice and his thoughts immediately side tracked to the dog tags usually dangling from Ariel's neck. They were missing tonight, replaced by a delicate diamond pendant. He decided it was time to penetrate her protective shell a little deeper. He didn't know why but every time he got close, she raised a shield. It wasn't unfriendly or rude, but politely professional. He was all about getting to the bottom of things. Diving in he asked, "So, your Dad was a Marine. Where did he serve?"

"Vietnam mostly, but his last deployment sent him to Lebanon." She touched her neck, dropped her hand with a jerk and looked at him sheepishly. "Talk about old habits."

"The dog tags?" he questioned.

"Yeah, they belonged to my father. He was stationed in Beirut when terrorists blew up the Marine barracks. The dog tags were recovered but nothing else..." She stared at her lap.

A waiter approached handing each of them a menu. Oblivious to the conversation, he rattled off his spiel about the special features of the day, took their drink order, and left.

Gavin ducked his hand under the table and grabbed her fingers, giving them a gentle squeeze. "I get it Ariel. I know about what happened in Beirut. I studied it when I was at Coronado as part of my training. Let me guess, you wear the tags to remind you freedom isn't free? Or something similar?"

"No, I wear them to remind myself of what my family lost, forever." The volume of her voice crept up. "I wear them to remind myself what's at stake if I fall in love with a military man."

Gavin's gut constricted as if he'd received a fisted punch. It all suddenly made sense. The way she'd avoided him. Rather than retreat he advanced. "Then I have to ask, what are you doing here, with me?"

She looked him straight in the eye. "Having dinner."

The waiter returned with two over-sized glasses of red wine and asked, "Are you ready to order?"

Gavin could have ordered shit on a stick for all he cared at this particular moment but he managed to ask for veal after Ariel ordered pasta, and then curtly excused the server. He soaked in the stunning woman across from him and tried not to say what was on his mind. Honestly, she took his breath away. He definitely desired more than a meal. So much more.

"I was three years old when my father was killed but he's still my hero." She began, her voice low and monotone. "He rose to Major in the Marine Corps and was scheduled to join the reserves at the end of 1983. Right before he left for Beirut, he informed my mother the mission would be his last deployment. She claimed he wanted to spend time at home participating in his kids' lives. My Dad was in the barracks when the bomb exploded."

Her gaze remained steady, her face void of any emotion, as she sat silently, apparently waiting for him to respond. He could only imagine the heartache she endured, witnessing her mother's suffering and her own longing for a father she only remembered from pictures. His eyes locked on hers. As a combat vet, he'd become immune to observing suffering and death but nothing impacted him like perceiving the tiny quiver erupting on her chin as she held back what he imagined was a tidal wave of emotions. He touched her hands clasped together on the tabletop, gently unfolding her fingers and intertwining them with his own. He lightly rubbed his calloused thumb across the tops of her smooth knuckles and guessed what she might be thinking.

She offered up a smile locking her fingers in his embrace. "The waiter should be here soon with our food. I don't know about you but I'm starved." She leaned close enough to his mouth so his breath exhaled on her lips and whispered, "I'm okay Gavin, honest, but thanks for listening to me. It's been a long time since I revealed my personal story to anyone."

As if on cue, the waiter showed up toting a tray of steaming plates piled high with garlic-laced veal and linguine smothered in marinara sauce.

All he could think as he stuck his fork in the veal was how much he admired the indomitable spirit sitting across from him. No way would he inflict any additional angst in her life. The stark reality loomed she was the poster child for his personal pledge. He framed the promise because he didn't want a trio of officers walking up his driveway to break the news Daddy wasn't coming home to his wife and children. In spite of the treasure trove of feelings Ariel induced in him, he needed to keep the relationship in perspective; they were simply having dinner.

****

As they stood face to face under the dim glow of the front porch light, Ariel didn't want the date to end. Scary thought considering she'd spent the evening with a guy who hunted down terrorists for a living. Even scarier idea, she actually enjoyed spending time with this particular man, a military man. She sensed he wanted to linger. "You want to come in for a glass of wine?"

He replied without hesitation, "Sure. It's not like I have to drive home."

Ariel giggled at his tongue-in-cheek humor as she unlocked the door. He squeezed into her space, so close his warm breath caressed her neck, exciting and fluffing the hair on her arms. She froze. Turning around would reveal the heat she was sure burned in her eyes. Instead, she rubbed her arms up and down as if chilled by the night air. But chilled was the last sensation she was experiencing. Her whole body quivered with want and need for this man. Resolved to keep it friendly, but not wanton sex friendly, she breezed through the opening and headed straight for the kitchen.

"So," she asked quietly, handing him a glass of wine, "I've spilled my guts to you, so to speak. How about a little reciprocation?"

He cleared his throat, "I'm an open book. What do you want to know?"

Everything, but the word stuck in her throat. Distracted by the unmistakable clench in her feminine region, she stared at the male perfection leaning casually against the kitchen counter, sipping his wine. The charcoal gray suit changed his appearance from ruggedly handsome to scorching, GQ hot. His broad shoulders filled out the jacket like it was tailored-made for him. Her belly tightened as he pushed off the ledge, tossed the remaining wine down his throat, and winked at her. *What the heck?* She sensed the evening was about to become even more interesting when he put his glass in the sink and gripped his tie.

His muscles flexed as he tugged the cloth back and

forth to loosen its hold. With a final tug, he untied the knot and placed the tie on the counter. He opened the top button of the baby blue shirt he wore freeing dark brown swirls of hair, which peeked out from the open V.

"All of it," she finally found her voice and sighed out loud, breathless from arousal. Sure the heat rising in her cheeks would give her away, she started to turn but the problematic man she had resisted so strenuously was already a step ahead. Her fingers trembled as he seized her wine glass and set it aside. He grabbed Ariel's hand and steered her to the overstuffed sofa in the adjacent living room. He sat first, and with a curl of his index finger, invited her next to him.

"You want reciprocation, baby?" He probed in a devilish tone, swiping the young doctor's hair behind her ear. "You have the most beautiful neck I've ever seen," he breathed deeply and whispered, as he began placing tender, slow kisses in the crook of her neck. Working his way up he murmured, "I deem this face exquisite," and placed a light kiss on the tip of her nose.

She sensed the smile on his lips and sighed with pleasure, "Well, Mr. SEAL, you have me rethinking my definition of reciprocation."

"Good to know," he said, his nose caressing her cheek. "Cause I like my definition better."

Ariel licked her lips in anticipation of hot kisses tantalizing her mouth. "Umm, me too." She jerked on his jacket sleeves, a half smile on her face. "You wouldn't want to wrinkle this nice suit, would you?"

****

Determined to take it slow he didn't react as fire alarms dinged in his head but God almighty she drove him crazy. Frozen in place, he allowed her control, while she extracted him from the suit jacket and tossed it on the nearby chair. "No, ma'am. Don't want any wrinkles in this activity." He wondered if she picked up on the double entendre.

As she began unfastening the buttons of his collared, starched shirt, working from the bottom up, he drawled, "Don't want to mess this shirt up either."

Ariel continued releasing the buttons, her cheeks flushed. "No way," she said amicably, as her hands hungrily hit the top of the row and stripped the shirt off him, flinging it to the side.

To hell with slow and careful. Gavin nimbly shifted Ariel's body so her legs straddled him and her bottom rested invitingly on his crotch. He craved access to every part of her sumptuous body.

He stretched up for a kiss. Ariel responded by slightly parting her lips. Accepting the invitation, he thrust his tongue in her sweet mouth and found hers waiting for him, eager and receptive. They tangled together and explored every corner, the tips flicking in and out. Gavin corralled Ariel's tongue and sucked it deeper into his own mouth. She responded by teasing her bosom into his chest, signaling a desire for more. Gavin seized the zipper on the back of the sexy raven-colored dress and in one smooth motion, slid it all the way down her back, off her arms until it settled around her waist. The ivory swell of skin undulating over the top of her lacy black bra ignited a primal need so sweet and delicious he groaned in anticipation. Longing to savor her breasts in his mouth, sucking and nipping and kissing each one in turn, he repositioned the hand still resting in the curve of Ariel's back up to the clasp of her bra and released the hooks. Ariel slid the straps off her shoulders, down her arms, and tossed the under garment on the floor.

Gavin's gut clenched. "Do you have any idea how much I want you?" he murmured.

Ariel let out a slow, soft whistle at the hardening bulge between his legs and nodded in affirmative, gently fondling his package. "Those pants look kinda tight. They definitely need to come off."

Gavin eagerly grabbed the zipper but Ariel touched his hand and smiled, "Let me."

His breath hitched as she slowly tugged the zipper down. "Careful, I'm dressed commando." Her stare turned steamy as her gaze drifted down. "Careful it is." She smirked as she sneaked her free hand inside his pants and wasted no time freeing his manhood.

With her eyes locked on his, she backed off the sofa and shimmied out of her dress, letting it puddle on the floor at her feet. Positioned directly in front of him, naked except for her black lace panties, she kicked free of the fabic and offered her outstretched hand to help him up.

Gavin locked his hand in hers and bounded to his feet, hopping from one foot to the other as he stripped off his pants. Desire coiled in his belly as Ariel's eyes locked on to his full, hard erection, unhampered by the constraints of his trousers. He gently lifted her chin and kissed her slowly, melting into the softness of her puckered lips. His manhood pressed unencumbered against her belly making his lascivious intention clear as he hugged her tighter.

She returned the intimacy by clutching his buttocks and grinding into him. "You're accompanied by a little foiled friend, aren't you?" Her voice smoldered.

Any self-control Gavin still possessed blew out the door. "Oh baby," he moaned as he grabbed a small packet from his pants pocket and placed it in his teeth. Gavin lifted Ariel in his arms and headed for the bedroom. He'd never wanted anyone as much as he wanted her right now.

Ariel wrapped her arms around his neck, laid her head on his thick shoulder and inhaled. "I love the way you smell, all seductive, musky, and masculine."

"Never heard my scent described like that before but I like it," he mumbled with the packet clenched between his teeth.

She sighed in what sounded like complete submission, "Are we there yet? I want you inside me."

Gavin's jaw clenched with obvious commitment to the task at hand. His bold determination to make love to her fanned the flame of desire into a roaring bonfire as he reached the top of the stairs and navigated the short hallway. He passed sideways through the door of the master bedroom with his precious cargo and gently laid her on the suede throw topping the bed.

"All night long, baby. You can have me all night long." He fell headlong next to her.

Her lips curved up in anticipation as her gaze travelled up and down his body, admiring the perfect nakedness from head to toe. "You definitely look up to the challenge."

He expelled a half laugh as he hooked his thumbs into each side of her underwear and smoothly stripped off her black lacy panties. "You're a funny girl," he hesitated and in a sultry baritone voice continued, "and a beautiful woman." Gavin rolled to face the woman from whom he'd sworn to stay away. He hugged her closer so his groin could thrust against her feminine curls. He fondled her fit body along every curve, all the way to her inviting center. As he licked the tips of her taut nipples in firm strokes, she writhed beneath him. Fueled by her arousal, he curled his mouth alternately around each darkened center, nipping and sucking.

Ariel mewed in ecstasy and spread her legs. She gripped the moist head of his fully extended member and slid her hand up and down caressing the taunt skin, stroke after slow, even stroke. "Now Gavin, I need you now," she moaned, urging him toward her willing entrance.

He twisted at the waist, extending his arm behind him so as not to break contact and grabbed the small foil square he'd dropped on the bedside table. Ariel snatched it out of his hand and ripped off the top. With exquisite care she unrolled its contents onto his erection. He gave her a wicked smile and shifted to mount her. She returned the grin, her eyes glazing over as he poked her opening, his enlarged member pulsating. He slid inside and her center tightened, her urgency adding to his excitement, making his start with even, slow strokes, a test of his self-discipline.

"Please," she breathed, her escalating desire obvious.

He willingly plunged to the hilt sending their pleasure meters off the dial.

Ariel enfolded her hands in his hair elevating her hips, meeting each thrust, each drive, her sublime expression a testament to the unbearably intense pleasure. She closed her eyes and mouthed the word, "ecstasy," as her orgasm throbbed around Gavin's engorged member. He held on, squeezing her hips against his groin as if the intensity could climb any higher. He pumped hard and fast until his control finally shattered. He emptied his seed inside her. It was the moment of truth. And the truth was this was the best sex he'd ever had. It all boiled down to the fact he had feelings for her. Serious feelings, unlike any he'd had before.

****

Ariel rolled over and snuggled closer to the amazing man asleep next to her. The man with whom he had shared the decadence of complete gratification. She no longer cared about Gavin's career choice. The fact he soldiered for a living didn't matter. She peered up at him and soaked in the simple splendor of his peaceful face, almost a smile on his beckoning lips. She propped up on an elbow and his eyes opened, her discreet motion triggering his hyper aware senses.

Instantly alert and awake, he pored over her face with a partial smile turned into a slow, cheeky grin. "Morning baby," he purred hoarsely, his fingers lightly stroking her thigh. "Hungry?"

She smiled, "Yeah, but not for bacon and eggs." God she felt naughty and naughty felt good. Arms wide, she closed her eyes and dove straight into his chest, deeply inhaling the scent of the man who pleasured her soul-deep. She was a goner but she didn't care. Right now, in this moment, she was happy. All the hardship and worry she fought so hard to keep constantly under control melted away as Gavin stroked her back with his rough broad hands, up and down. She moaned as his caresses extended to her bottom. He kneaded each cheek in confirmation her buttocks were his favorite part of her anatomy. She preferred a certain part of him too, and extended her hand between his legs to reciprocate.

"Doctor Armstrong, you drive me crazy," he responded as she dipped her head down to replace her hand with her eager mouth. "Babe, you're gonna have me come undone," Gavin groaned, tilting his head. "I love watching your masterful oral technique but things are about to come to an abrupt end." He gently lifted her up and on top of him.

"You want me to stop?" she asked.

"No way." He grunted as he maneuvered her over him. "Just show me a little mercy, will you?" He laughed.

"No mercy for you, G." She smirked as she sank to his base and pumped in driven delight. She sensed him give way, no longer able to maintain control as they tumbled over the cliff together. No doubt about it, he lit her world on fire.

****

Ariel stood at the stove scrambling eggs and dodging the bacon grease popping out of the frying pan. She listened to the water turn on in the shower upstairs. She never planned to have her comfort zone so pleasantly exploited, especially by a man like Gavin. But here she was, breaking all her own rules. It wasn't just sex anymore. She experienced a natural sense of ease around him. Instinctively her heart told her, he was someone she could trust. Honestly, she didn't know where they were headed but one thing was for sure, she could get hurt. No, she could get decimated by a relationship with Mr. Frogman. The pulsating sound of shower water stopped. "He'll be swash buckling into the kitchen any minute. What's my plan?" She muttered aloud. "I really need a plan." Her stomach tightened as he tiptoed up behind her and placed a sweet kiss on her neck.

"Something smells good. I'm famished." He breathed into her ear.

Her body tensed and he instantly backed away. Yep, it was one more indicator they were riding the same emotional wave, she realized, as she handed him a plate of bacon and eggs.

"Everything okay?" he asked, his brow furrowed.

"No, it's not ok." She hesitated, taking in his troubled look, "It's perfect and perfect worries me."

"Wait a minute. Perfection is good, right? I don't get it. What's bothering you?" He pinned her with his glacier blue eyes.

Intimidated by his intensity, she studied the floor, silent.

"Oh, I get it. The, 'I'm off limits because I'm a military man,' consideration again."

"No, actually I'm reconsidering the decision," she replied softly, gazing at him.

Gavin dug his fork into a pile of eggs. "What then?"

"It feels like a week ago but I want to ask you about the night before last."

It was the question he'd been bracing himself for and realized it couldn't be avoided any longer so he faced her. "Shoot."

"What do you remember about the," she didn't know what to call it, "event?"

"Not a thing," Gavin said as evenly as he could. "Absolutely nada. When I woke up it seemed like a dream so I blew it off. I know it's hard to believe but I'm telling you the truth."

"Have you talked to anyone else about what happened?"

"I talked to my Dad about it yesterday afternoon."

"Oh, how did it go?" She believed him. He looked so earnest.

"Not so well. As a matter of fact, horrible." He plopped down on the kitchen stool, stuffed a piece of bacon in his mouth, and stared out the nearby window as if transfixed in thought.

Ariel could see from the sadness on his face, the sting of the encounter was fresh. She shifted to stand next to him and propped her hip on his leg, placing her hand on his knee. "What happened?"

"Dad laid the Navy point of view out for me but I didn't want to hear the truth. I shut him down, believing he was on their side, and stormed off." He looked sheepishly at Ariel.

"Gavin, you can fix things with your father. Not only is he very logical and rational but my bet is he understands how you feel and supports you." She rubbed his knee. "Unconditionally." She finished and stood quietly. She sensed there was more.

He nodded his agreement. "Apparently, the reigning powers in the Navy have decided I have some form of PTSD." He shook his head in frustration. "And in order to remain on the Teams I have to submit to therapy and a possible psych evaluation.. Then, engage in whatever dog and pony show the doctor determines will fix me. As much as I want to be on the teams, I don't want to submit to someone tinkering with my head. I'm a SEAL dammit. We are screened out for

PTSD. I never imagined I had a breaking point but isn't this some shit? If I go through with the therapy, I'll never live it down with the guys. You know I fell for the ruse I was being sent home for R&R due to the strenuous schedule our assignment required. My friend and the Team corpsman, Tony, put me on a plane home, smiling and waving like it was a holiday. Why wasn't he straight with me?"

Even with horses the doctor dealt with resistance to treatment. The best course of action was calm control and a lot of resolve to administer the correct medicine. "Maybe he predicted how you'd react, so in the best tradition of friendship, he hornswoggled you." She tilted her head and grinned at him. The levity worked.

Gavin's face relaxed. "Yeah, I guess I'm still a bit upset over finding out from my father I drew a gun on Tony. What a load of shit, Ariel. I was sleepwalking like the other night and don't remember a thing. I'm not convinced seeing a shrink is the best course of action."

She intentionally ignored his last comment but her tone changed to serious, "Do you know what the treatment plan entails?"

"Other than shrink-wrapping? Not exactly." He looked down for a second before he looked her straight in the eye. "The truth is I'm afraid he'll recommend the Navy off load me on a medical discharge. What if he can't fix me?"

There it was in a nutshell. The complex man standing in front of her would rather suffer endlessly with his illness than seek help, which could potentially land him out of the Navy. But if he didn't get treatment, he was out. It was a perfect problem. She sighed. If she listened to her heart, she'd steer him toward leaving the

SEAL Teams. It would resolve her dilemma of a military free zone in her personal life. But if she consulted her head, a lesson from her Marine Corp father popped up. It was simple. You could take the man out of the military but you couldn't take the military out of the man. Gavin would die being a Navy SEAL, whether it was in a year or at a ripe old age. Ariel resolved what she had to do.

With her hands on either side of his chiseled face, she bent down to kiss him. He reacted immediately, kissing her back with an intensity requiring her to let go of his face and grip his shoulders. Tears rolled uncontrollably down her face as she mentally cemented her decision. Their tongues intertwined with the salty taste of her crying but the emotion only contributed to the intimate pleasure she tightly wrapped herself in with this man.

Ariel reluctantly broke the embrace but kept her lips a millimeter away from Gavin's mouth.

Breathless, she whispered, "G, you can be fixed. No 'easy day' though. It's going to take a lot of hard work but I believe in you. I know you're getting back on the Teams."

Chapter 13

Ariel always welcomed the elusive day off in her line of work. Horses didn't make appointments for medical care and with uncanny frequency their emergencies cropped up on the weekends or in the middle of the night. With uncleaned breakfast dishes left in the sink, she let the screen door slam behind her as she made a beeline for her truck, her treat to herself on a sunny Sunday to do whatever she pleased.

Some distance from the whirlwind of events and jumble of emotions created by the recent circumstances was exactly what the doctor ordered, for herself.

Truthfully, she wanted some space from Gavin. The prospect of taking on the commitment to help him heal, so he could plunge back into harm's way, was daunting, but combined with her pledge to oversee John's care...well, the idea of flood waters overwhelming a dam came to mind. Thinking of her beloved brother, a road trip to Jacksonville was what the doctor ordered, for herself. It was another beautiful August day in Florida, perfect to cruise an uncrowded highway. Standing next to her truck, she tilted her head skyward and shielded her eyes from the intense southern sun with one hand, while retrieving her favorite pair of sunglasses from her purse with her other hand. Puffy low-hung clouds dotted the sun-drenched sky. She loved the Florida summers in spite of the clinging humidity because relief from the heavy air inevitably rolled in as rain, warmed by the Gulf currents, along with a dazzling light show from lightning and ear-deafening thunder. You could set your watch by the afternoon storms and somehow the predictability of nature's cycle gave the Florida convert comfort. Yes, a heartfelt conversation with her most trusted childhood confidant seemed like a perfect way to spend the much-needed time off.

Ariel dug into her purse for her keys and climbed in. She adjusted the rear view mirror using it to capture a view of the stable, certain Gavin worked inside, as the truck bumped down the unpaved driveway in the opposite direction, toward Jacksonville.

****

Ariel punched the elevator button for John's floor, then stepped back to watch the lighted knob ding its way to the lobby. She toyed with her plastic visitor's badge as she waited for the door to open. *My brother is going to enjoy hearing the latest escapade in my love life. He'll probably be amused I've chosen him as my confidant.*

They had been joint conspirators in helping each other escape discovery from their mother growing up but as adults it suddenly seemed odd to Ariel, she'd confide her passions to her little brother. She usually shared all items in the romance department with her closet friend, Sierra. But she had an ulterior motive. Her last phone call from Dr. Remington Lewis indicated his patient's recovery was advancing well ahead of target. He recommended involving John in as much normal activity as possible to help him transition to outside life. Well, relaying the events of the past few days would certainly contribute to the idea of involving him but the normal part might be a stretch.

The elevator door slid open. She stepped in first, shifting to the back of the small space as other waiting passengers shuffled in behind her. The ride to the fourth floor was quiet while each person probably pondered the outcome for the loved one they were visiting. The chime sounded and the doors slid apart allowing everyone to unload. She stepped off and headed down the hall, eager to check on John's progress and share her own version of Entertainment Tonight.

"Dr. Armstrong, this is a nice surprise."

Dr. Lewis looked as luscious as ever in his white lab coat and tennis shoes, Ariel decided as she stuck her hand into his offered grip. "Likewise, Doctor."

"It's Remington, remember?" He winked.

"I know you're here to see John so I'll walk you to his room." He gently touched her arm and smiled. "It'll give us a chance to talk." He gestured with his hand indicating for her to go ahead of him.

"Always the gentleman." She smiled and stepped forward. "Actually, I'd like to discuss another topic, if you have a minute."

"Absolutely, whatever you need."

He kept his doctor face on but his "absolutely" seemed a bit eager to Ariel. The way he looked at her had not gone unnoticed and under other circumstances, like she hadn't entered the SEAL kingdom by having glorious sex with Gavin, she'd pursue the potential with enthusiasm.

"Well, it's not a subject I know much about but I'm hoping you can offer some enlightenment."

Okay, now his doctor face was off and he was

staring.

"PTSD," she blurted out and stopped.

"You think you have PTSD?" he asked, observably puzzled.

"Not me," she hesitated, "a—friend of mine recently back from Afghanistan." She shifted on her feet, uncomfortable, as the handsome doctor scrutinized her face. "He's been involved in a lot of combat including heavy fire fights."

"Well, as a doctor who works at the Naval Hospital, I've dealt with plenty of PTSD patients so I'm aware of the basic symptoms. What are his symptoms?"

Ariel trusted him. She couldn't go it alone, so without mincing words, she detailed the recent sleep walking episode, gesturing with her hands, eyes wide, and her face scrunched in worry. She noticed the fine lines around Remington's eyes wrinkle into a concerned wince but he listened intently without interrupting. She finished her story by outing Gavin's reluctance to seek help.

Remington let out a low whistle. "The guy sounds like a controlled riot."

"I'd say, 'controlled' and 'riot' combined aptly describe his current situation," she said in agreement. "Remington, you get it," she sighed with relief.

"As a start, I can refer you to a colleague of mine, a neurologist, right here at the Naval Hospital who specializes in PTSD cases. He is a Navy vet with first-hand experience," Remington assured Ariel. "Suffice it to say he understands the issue. I also have a few articles in my office I'll loan you so you have reliable information about the topic before you meet him." He finished by placing his hand on her shoulder. "Ariel, I admire you for wanting to help your friend but he sounds dangerous and in trouble which could make any involvement with him risky. I'd avoid any emotional entanglement with him until he receives the benefit of treatment and becomes a little more stable."

Too late, I'm in chin deep. "I appreciate the warning, Remington, but I can take care of myself."

His eyes pierced her with a hard stare. "Make sure you do. John's counting on your support and quite frankly, his well-being matters to me," his voice soft, "as does yours."

Heat rose up her neck and covered her face. "I want to assure you John is my undisputed priority." *Is he flirting with me?* "And I'm flattered you're concerned about my well-being, truly, but I'm okay." She rocked back on her heels, shoving her hands in her jean's pockets and started for the closed door of her brother's room. "Let's check on John." She leaned around the corner of the doorframe and peeked in. "He's asleep," she mouthed over her shoulder.

Remington lightly encouraged her forward, skimming her back with his palm. "Sit next to him so you're there when he wakes up. He'd like having your face as his first vision. I have rounds to do but I'll drop by before I leave and answer any questions you have."

Ariel stood on her tiptoes and planted a chaste kiss on the doctor's cheek, "Thanks for caring about us."

"You bet." He winked at her and then disappeared down the hallway into another patient's room.

Ariel found a comfortable chair by the window and plopped down. She looked at John while he slept. He was handsome and looked remarkably like the pictures she'd seen of her father as a young lieutenant. As if to verify the resemblance, she grabbed her wallet from her purse and retrieved the single small photo she always carried of him. He had recently made Major and the broad smile on his face evidenced his pride for the accomplishment. She peered out at the well-manicured grounds as her thoughts drifted back to the day her world turned upside down. The incident was seared in her mind like a tattoo and Ariel remembered every vivid detail.

She had finished breakfast and after insisting her imaginary friend, Chantilly, also finish eating, she padded into the living room to a safe play area. She gathered her dolls into a corner and one by one lined them up against the sofa for an art class. Determined to teach them how to draw a circle, she instructed Chantilly to show them first. The sharp thud of three car doors shutting in succession startled her and interrupted the lesson. She scampered to the picture window climbing up on the wide curving ledge, curious to investigate who was visiting them. Two stern looking men, accompanied by a woman, dressed in fancy blue with red trim uniforms, walked solemnly, eyes straight ahead, toward the front door. Ariel remembered her stomach feeling sick and an urgent need to locate her mother for reassurance. She scrambled off the sill as the doorbell tolled twice. She called out for her mama as she tore down the short hallway following the tic tac of her mother's shoes on the wood floor and skidded to a stop in front of two boat-sized shiny black shoes. The owner bent down on one leg and patted her head while the lady talked in a whispered voice to her mother. The second man stood stiffly by the front door, like he wanted to leave. The more the woman spoke, the tighter

Mama's face scrunched up in a big frown. What was the lady saying to her mother? Mama's shoulders started to quiver and tears cascaded down her cheeks. She planted her face in her hands and moaned, "Oh God no. This isn't happening." Mama's knees buckled and she placed her right hand protectively onto her swollen stomach. The man by the door leapt forward catching her by the elbow. He wrapped his arm around her waist and guided Mama's limp body to the sofa. Is something wrong with the baby she wondered, confused at her mother's distress? Her young heart pounded against her rib cage and pressure filled her chest. The tall man in the shoes extended his hand palm up. She tightly gripped his index finger as he ushered her across the room where Mama sat shaking her head back and forth, her eyes staring out the window. She placed her chubby hand on her mama's knee to comfort her but Mama didn't respond. Desperate to help, she climbed up on the couch and touched her mama's rounded stomach, making small circles on the surface, encouraging the baby to be brave like Daddy. Mama bawled and bawled, her shoulders shaking with every sob. The two men and lady stayed all day with Mama. They comforted her, offered water, tissue, and prayer.

One good memory remained from the time. The next day and for many days after, the neighbors delivered food, drink, and kindness to their house. The day of the funeral they showed up in force, cooking, cleaning, and supporting her mother in every way. It cemented her life-long belief people are mostly good.

The main recollection she retained from the funeral consisted of a single line her mother said. "Your Daddy isn't coming home, ever." She didn't remember the rest of the explanation. It was difficult for a three year old to wrap her wits around 'forever' but the overwhelming sadness in her mother's face said it all. It was longer than her mother could bear.

Ariel fortified a subconscious decision on that fateful day. She would sidestep monumental suffering like her mother had experienced and avoid romantic entanglements with a military man.

She glanced back at her sleeping brother and remembered their discussions about him joining the Marines and her unsuccessful attempts to talk him out of it but he, unlike his sister, had not been traumatized by their father's death. He grew up with the single-minded belief his father was a hero. All he dreamed of was emulating his idol by joining the Marine Corp. He'd done so in spades.

"Hey Sis, how long have you been sitting here?"

The sound of her brother's voice brought Ariel back to the present and she mentally shook off the memories. "Oh, good morning, Pest. Not long. Have a good sleep?" she said affectionately, as she ruffled his hair.

"Yeah, I must have really gone 'zero dark thirty' from the pain meds," he said with a grin, playfully swatting at her hand.

"Doc says you're okay to go outside? It's a perfect summer day in Florida. Swelter is at plus ten. Interested?"

John strained his gaze toward the window but the neck brace kept his head from turning.

"Yeah, the heat couldn't be any worse than the climate in Afghanistan and I don't have sixty pounds of gear to lug around. I'm game."

"You must be a little groggy after being asleep for a few hours. I'll get an orderly to help you into your chariot, master," she teased, climbing reluctantly out of the comfy chair.

He laughed, "Well, it's not like I'm going anywhere without my throne."

She smiled and nodded as she exited the room unable to pester him with a catchy comeback due to the lump lodged in her throat. He was without question the bravest person she'd ever met. John still had a lot to offer in this life and she'd make damn sure every opportunity was afforded him to achieve his own version of greatness. She gazed down the long hall for someone to help her lift him into the wheel chair. A well-muscled young man in blue scrubs immediately headed in her direction. "He fits the bill," she declared.

"Do you need assistance?" The man offered an easy smile.

"Yes, I could use help getting my brother into his wheel chair." Ariel glanced at the room door behind her.

"Oh, Lt. Armstrong? Whatever he needs, ma'am." The man's tone indicated noticeable respect as he passed Ariel and entered the room.

He greeted John with Semper Fi and a toothy grin. He grabbed the wheel chair from the corner, positioned it directly next to the bed, and efficiently lifted John's broken body over to the chair.

"Thanks, man." John grunted as he used his arms and adjusted his physique to a more upright position.

"Anytime, lieutenant. Enjoy the fresh air," he replied before turning to speed off down the hallway.

"I didn't realize you were such a hot shot, little

brother." Ariel bantered, as pride in her sibling bubbled up. "I'm very proud of you. I hope you know you're a hero." She choked as the last word rolled over the lump in her throat. Moisture filled her eyes. *God, don't choke Ariel. Keep it light.*

John joked, offering her an escape, "Well, *doctor*, back at you. Both brains and beauty render a deadly combo. Don't think I haven't noticed every male within staring distance, checking out my hot sister."

"Huh?" Ariel gave it her best, cross-eyed, 'who me' face, before breaking into a chuckle.

"C'mon, Doc, you know exactly what I'm talking about. I'll give you a hint. My Marine buddies can't make a complete sentence when you come around. You need further proof? I've got more."

Ariel seized the handles of the wheel chair, propelled it forward out of the room and down the hall to the elevator. "No, knuckle-head. I get it. But they're your jarhead buddies. They check out any breathing female under forty."

"Geez, you're funny in an annoying kind of way." He volleyed back, sending her one of his most wicked grins.

Ariel wheeled her feisty, kid brother into the blinding glare of the Florida sunlight. "Ah, all is right in the universe again."

Chapter 14

"Well, my visit went better than expected," Ariel mused out loud as she backed her truck out of the Naval Hospital parking space. Her little brother didn't even feign shock or surprise at his sister's latest love exploits. In fact, his face relaxed with a perceptible contentment when she told him she was leaning like the Tower of Pisa toward something serious with a Navy SEAL. He expressed a certain regard for them he'd never voiced before, at least not to her. It was a level of respect he usually reserved for the Marines. Of course, she left out the part about PTSD not to worry him. She also deleted any mention the military man was related to her boss. Details, Ariel reflected. John didn't need to be hampered in his own recovery with details. Her protective instincts kicked in as did her dogged determination, nothing would get in the way of his recuperation. The return of their shared banter was food for the soul and proof positive her brother maintained his optimistic attitude in spite of everything. She would be the gorilla at the gate where it concerned her little brother's welfare.

****

Ariel rolled up to the cottage, threw the gearshift into park, and grabbed for the door handle. Except, the door handle wasn't there. Gavin had yanked open the door and placed himself inside the compact opening, inches from her face, his eyes frosted over with anger. An impulsive shiver rolled down her arms as she recovered from the surprise and struggled for something witty to say.

Gavin saved her from the effort, "Hey, you've been gone all day." After stating the obvious he waited for her response.

"Yeah, it's my day off," she quipped. "Are you part Ninja? I didn't see or hear you come up to the truck."

"Part of the job requirements," he gave a clipped response. "And you were driving around with your doors unlocked. Not smart."

"I unlocked the door right before I stopped," she replied, undaunted by his insolence.

His mouth drew into a tight line. "Where'd you go on your day off?"

"Jacksonville, if you must know, which you obviously feel you do."

Unrelenting he continued, "What, or should I say who, is in Jacksonville?"

Ariel detected a sharp edginess in Gavin's behavior and instinctively sought to humor him. "Lots of shoe stores." She winked.

He instantly checked out her back seat. "I don't see any packages, Miss Smart-ass."

"Well, I didn't say I actually bought anything," she countered flippantly, observing his right jaw popping repeatedly. He offered no snarky comeback but simply stood there, arms crossed and muscles bulging like an impenetrable fortress.

Unable to lighten him up, Ariel decided to take the opposite tact and coax him into spitting out the true reason for giving her the third degree. She wanted to hear Gavin admit his jealousy. Although the idea of goading a man like Gavin was worrisome, being involved with another jealous man registered a ten on the uncomfortable scale. She'd been down this road before with her ex, Drake, and couldn't deal with another possessive, overbearing man. She refused to ever be intimidated again. Compelled by her past, she decided to teach the man scowling at her a lesson. "Well, there was and is a very important 'who.' I've wanted to tell you about him but I was waiting for the right time."

Surprise flooded his face before a frown creased his forehead. He balled his hands into fists, and then shoved them into his jeans pockets. He looked away and jiggled the loose change in his pocket. It was a nervous habit she'd witnessed before when he didn't know what else to do. *I believe I've made my point. Time to come clean.*

"I was at the Naval Hospital visiting my *brother*, tough guy. While we're at it, you should know I don't usually have casual sex with men or sleep around. I'm sorry if I gave you the wrong idea, you know, the other day, out in the pasture, and, uh, last night."

"No, Ariel, you didn't. I was simply concerned when you stayed gone all day."

What a cop-out. Determined not to let him off the hook, she queried, "Concerned? Is concern what you're calling this shake-down?"

"Yeah, concern is what I'm calling my questions, and it's not a shake down. There are a lot of bad people out there. Believe me, I'm an expert on Bad. Do you understand?"

"I totally do, but relationships are built on trust. It boils down to whether or not you really know who I am." She placed her hands on her hips. "And, if you *do*, you wouldn't worry about what I'm up to or who I'm with. Jealousy is the antithesis to trust, Mr. Bossy Frogman."

"Okay, now you're throwing big words at me, darlin'." He finally smiled. His face relaxed and he withdrew his hands from his pockets, dangling them loosely by his side.

"The Team guys are the only ones I've put my total reliance in, until now. I do trust you Ariel, but I admit I got a little worried, jealous, whatever, when you disappeared all day."

Talk about turning the tables. She couldn't think of any appropriate verbal response so she zeroed in on his perfect lips and kissed him.

He returned the kiss, caressing her mouth with delicious, feather-light strokes of his tongue bolstering her desire for more. She parted her lips, allowing his tongue entry to flick in and out of her mouth in what felt to her like a heated dance. Her mind numbed as he planted a deep, soulful, I-really-mean-it kiss in the curve of her neck. She fisted her hands in his hair and moaned, as the dizzy, hot sensation rolled to her groin. A wave of jumbled feelings washed over her. She'd never experienced emotions this raw or intense with anyone else. Splaying her palms on Gavin's chest, she broke the embrace and leaned back. "You're very seductive and I don't want to stop but you do realize where we are, right?"

Gavin, his eyes glazed over with obvious desire, skimmed her cheeks with his knuckles. "You're beautiful, Ariel."

"So are you, Frogman." She flushed.

"We're good, right?" he said with a lop-sided grin. "I noticed you dropped the Mr. and the bossy."

"All good, all the time."

"Uh, the saying is, 'All in all the time' but I get your drift. By the way, I didn't know you had a brother."

"Yeah, I have a brother. Your Dad didn't tell you?"

"No, he's big on 'need to know' and whatever information you've shared with him doesn't get shared with anyone else, including yours truly. And speaking of my father, he's headed this way."

Ariel spun around to see her favorite boss smiling and waving at them. She waved back, admiring the way he carried himself with such complete certainty. Jeff commanded respect without being overbearing and had an ability to exact the best out of everyone in his sphere of influence. "He looks happy. Does this mean you two repaired the misunderstanding?"

"Something close to a truce," Gavin replied out of the side of his mouth. "If you call telling him I'd look into making an appointment at the Naval Hospital Jacksonville. I guess the gesture acted as a peace offering. It got him to back off."

"Well, are you?" She raised her eyebrow giving him a questioning look.

"Am I what?" He turned both palms out and appeared clueless.

She poked him in the stomach with her index finger. "You're a rotten, awful man. You know you are, right?"

He casually placed one hand in the small of her

back without averting his focus from his approaching father.

"Does he know about us?" Ariel inquired with a whisper.

"Probably, but I want to make sure." He nudged her with his hip and winked.

"You're incorrigible." She stamped her foot, bumped him back harder, and stepped away disconnecting his hand from her waist.

As Jeff got closer, Ariel caught a knowing twinkle in his eye indicating he hadn't missed anything occurring on his farm. Nope, not a damn thing. She didn't care. The fact Jeff didn't tell Gavin about her brother proved his discretion and sewed up her trust in him.

Jeff spoke first, pretending formality, "Hi Doctor Armstrong, how was your day off?"

"It was kind of perfect Mr. Cross," she said, playing along. "In fact, I just got back."

"Well then, you haven't had time to fix dinner so you can join us for a cookout." It sounded more like a demand than a question, Jeff's version of politeness. Her stomach growled in agreement and she realized in her hasty departure for Jacksonville, she hadn't defrosted anything for supper. A noisy gurgle from her abdomen broadcast the needle was definitely on empty.

Ariel glanced at Gavin. He sent her a full on, 'yes I want you to come to dinner' smile.

She hooked her arm in Jeff's and turned them both toward the house. "Lead the way, boss."

Gavin fell in step on the other side of Ariel, head slightly bowed, hands in his pockets, quiet. He seemed unusually content listening to her regale his father with future plans for the foaling barn and their ultimate outcome of Kentucky Derby winners.

****

Gavin liked the way she behaved around his father, animated and alive, unlike when he'd first met her. His initial impression she was all business and honestly, a cold fish, turned out so wrong. She exuded warmth. All the guile and coy flirting he experienced in previous female encounters didn't exist with Ariel. She was down to earth, real, and oh so sexy. Her light brown hair, usually in a tight ponytail, flowed down her back today in deep waves flecked with sun-streaked highlights. It swayed back and forth with the swing of her hips. The skinny jeans she wore fit her exactly, so every curve was visible accenting her perfectly formed bottom. Her usual doctor smock was missing, replaced by a V-necked, periwinkle blue, cotton t-shirt which flattered her firm round breasts, showing just enough cleavage to drive him insane. His pants started to get tight around his crotch. Good thing he'd arrived at the picnic tables so he could sit down and hide the evidence of his arousal until the food arrived. He caught Ariel's eye and gave her the nod to come join him.

She nodded back and walked over smiling, "Ready to eat?"

He checked his crotch with his hand. "Yeah, lead the way." He stood up and swung his leg over the wood bench.

"Everything okay?" she chuckled, not oblivious to Gavin's predicament.

He raised an eyebrow in response and grabbed her hand, encouraging her forward toward the food table. The aroma of hickory smoked ribs wafted in the air and he lengthened his stride. Ariel's gait shifted into a slight jog to keep up but she didn't resist or complain. She adapted without acquiescing. Her show of tolerance was epic as far as he was concerned. A woman who could hold her own with him was what he'd wished for but always found elusive. He'd never met anyone as intoxicating as Doctor Sexy.

"Okay Marathon Man, grab a plate and dig in." Ariel jabbed him in the ribs as she lifted a plate from the stack and started down the line of platters filled with sizzling ribs, potato salad, homemade biscuits, and corn on the cob.

"Don't wait for me," he teased as he stabbed a rack of ribs with his fork and dropped it on his dinner-sized dish.

Gavin followed Ariel down the line, watching her select a sample taste from each platter until the desserts. She skipped over the pecan pie and chocolate cake like a champ and headed for the table they had staked out earlier. He decided her fit body wouldn't be harmed by a small slice of pie so he served two pieces on a separate plate and dropped them on the corner of his tray. He turned for the table and noticed Ariel was politely waiting for him before digging in to her pile of food.

He extended the tray toward her as he prepared to sit, happy with himself for offering her a dessert he was sure she wanted, but willfully resisted. "Look what the dessert fairy gifted you," he said, pointing to the slice of sweet indulgence. *Uh oh, she's giving me the stink eye.* He put the pie on the table.

"Gavin, if I wanted dessert I would have gotten dessert." She blew out a breath through her pursed lips.

"Don't you know how bad sugar is for you?"

"It's only one piece and the way you run around the farm, you'll burn through those calories in no time." Her nostrils flared. He was getting in too deep. *Time to shut up, dummy.* He slid the second piece of pie to his other side and smiled broadly. "All better?" he asked.

She jerked the plate back in front of her, "You're going to overdose if you eat both pieces Mr. Dessert Fairy, or should I call you, Dessert Devil?"

"Can I take one piece back?" he offered.

She stabbed her fork in the center of the pecans and lifted a bite straight into her mouth, "No you can't." She swallowed and licked her lips. "Ummm. Way too yummy to return," she giggled. "I was going to get dessert after I ate my meal but you are way too much fun to tease. Sorry G."

Grabbing her uneaten dessert he retorted, "No, you're not."

As if protecting a valuable from theft, she slapped his outstretched hand and snatched the dessert plate close to her chest. "Mine, all mine." She stuck her finger in the pie, sucked the filling off the tip and smacked her lips.

"Now, you've gone too far," he joked, leaping off the bench and diving over the top of the table sending utensils, food and plates flying. He seized the remaining pie from Ariel's hands, tossed it in his mouth, gulped it in one swallow, and licked all five fingers of his right hand.

The sound of clapping caught Gavin by surprise. He turned to see an appreciative crowd of onlookers gathered behind him. His father stood in front exuding his usual omnipresence. Their eyes met for a brief second before his Dad turned two thumbs up and joined the "woot, woot, woot," and the fist pumping.

"Holy shit." Gavin gawked at Ariel clutching the plate she'd caught mid-air, red sauce dripping down the front of her periwinkle shirt. He glanced down and witnessed his own food on the ground, covered in sand and grass. Too late to feel embarrassed, he figured a smart remark might prevent Ariel from breaking the plate she held over his hard head. "Guess the five second rule is out of the question. Want to share?"

"Sure," she flirted. Ariel sauntered around the corner of the table exaggerating the swing of her hips from side to side until she stood directly in front of the unsuspecting man. She scraped the gooey mess off her V-neck shirt with her index finger, intentionally leaving a spot on the edge of her cleavage. Gavin focused on the speck as she leaned in, sauce-covered finger extended. He opened his mouth in anticipation of her feeding him.

"Perfect," she said as she smeared the thick paste all over his face. "Pay back is hell, Dude," she giggled, quickly backing up.

Seemingly oblivious to the bright-colored paste covering his face, he focused on the pretty doctor. "Did you just call me Dude?"

Gavin's tone signaled retaliation, so she threw her plate at his head, turned, and raced toward the crowd for cover.

"You missed," he called gaining speed with every stride.

His footsteps pounded closer and in spite of her best efforts zig-zagging around the staff he caught her by the waistband of her jeans. Without breaking stride, he twirled her around and lifted her over his shoulder into a fireman's carry. From her recollection, they were headed straight for the swimming pool. "I have my good watch on," she yelled, hoping it would be a deterrent.

"Better take it off," he responded matter-of-factly.

She did the only thing left. She kicked her feet in the air and pounded her fists on his back until he jumped, legs bicycling, from the side of the pool. They floated airborne for a brief second, enough time for her to clamp her fingers across her nose and hear Gavin yell, "Hooyah," before butt-flopping into the deep end.

Chapter 15

Attired in a dry change of clothes, Gavin stared, mesmerized, while Ariel dried her hair with a towel she retrieved from her bathroom. Today's events had further piqued his interest in the stunning woman who, he discovered, possessed a fully developed sense of humor. When they floated to the pool's surface, he was certain she'd be furious and started to apologize but instead, she splashed a mouthful of water in his face. Then, she raced for the pool stairs and might have beaten him but a fit of giggles possessed her and she had to dog paddle in the final stretch. As he stroked past her, she made a feeble attempt to dunk him but missed and slapped the water. Besides, how do you out swim a frogman? You'd have to be another frogman.

A loud gurgle churned from his stomach and reminded him he hadn't eaten. "Hey Babe, are you still hungry?"

"Still hungry?" She cocked her head and kept drying her damp hair. "You're kidding right? Wager is the only one in this room who isn't starving."

Gavin kneeled and stroked the top of the collie's head. "I see your point. The little thief made out big time from our food fight." As if agreeing, Wager licked his chops, wagged his tail, and sat, looking expectantly at his owner for more ribs to be dropped on the ground. With a gentle swat to Wager's hind side, Gavin stood keeping his smile in place as he refrained from calling the canine a hair missile. *Enough lines had been crossed with the good doctor for one week.*

"I'll locate the leftovers while you finish up." He delivered his most boy-next-door grin. "It's the least I can do." His stomach growled so forcefully, Wager tilted his head in the direction of the noise.

She rolled her eyes and tapped her foot, conspicuously checking her watch. "Better hustle your behind, Mister," she teased. "You don't want to hear my stomach's call of the wild."

He shuffled out the door feeling like a high school sophomore. How alive can one man feel? Whatever brutal realities his situation obligated him to face were outweighed by having Ariel in his life. She was a calming salve on his emotional wounds. With her joining his cause, he could confront anything.

****

"Am I forgiven?" Gavin asked tossing his napkin on the empty plate.

"You are so forgiven," she licked barbeque sauce from the corner of her mouth and winked, "you can even spend the night, if you want."

He wiggled his eyebrows, "I want." *And want and want…in fact he'd never wanted anyone as much as he wanted the sexy woman in front of him.*

"Sounds good to me, G, but I need to check on a couple of mares before we call it a night. You and your one track mind can wait here if you want."

"It's called focus, darlin'." He sent her a devilish smile.

"Whatever you say." She gazed up at him and batted her eyelashes.

"So, what's happening with the mares important enough for you to venture out into the dark and stormy night?" he joked, his burden lightened by her good nature.

"I'm checking to see if they're ready for the stallion, and it's perfectly cloudless outside, Mr. Wise Guy. For your information, timing is everything with a live cover-breeding program, and these mares have had trouble getting pregnant in the past. We schedule the breeding so the sperm are patiently waiting for the egg to migrate down. I usually check on them earlier in the day but with all the pool sports we've been playing, I fell behind schedule."

"Well, I guess we better get moving. My sperm aren't so patient," he said, provocatively.

"Geez, you are so preoccupied with, with…"

"With you, Sunshine." He laughed as he held the door open. "Hope you don't mind a little company tonight cause I'm coming with you."

She answered with a punch to his deltoid and a coy smile as she slid past.

"No telling what trouble we can discover in the barn, among the piles of hay with only equine eyes watching." He swatted her behind as the screen door slammed shut behind them.

****

Jeff decided to check one last fence before the shadows of night eclipsed the remaining daylight. He had hoped he'd be finished by now. He should turn back. The country provided no illumination from city lights and the description 'pitch black' became literal. Fortunately, the night gifted him with the pearlescent glow of a full moon. As he ascended the steep hill overlooking the barnyard, he noticed the glimmer of headlights traveling down a secondary road along the outside perimeter of the farm. Always on alert for horse thieves he eased behind a large oak tree and waited. He remained motionless, as the vehicle drew near.

When the car arrived, parallel to his position, he could tell by the silhouette there was no trailer attached and started to head back down the hill. *Teenagers scouting a make-out location,* he mused. The older man placed one foot in front of the other, taking care not to trip over the exposed roots and uneven ground, wishing he'd had the foresight to grab a flashlight. He stopped his descent when the engine quit and turned in time to see the headlights go dark. A thickly built male exited the car, gripping a small dark bag. He ambled to the front of his car and raised both hands, staring intently, his attention focused straight ahead. The moon caught the reflection of the glass.

What the hell? Are those binoculars? What could he possibly be surveilling? I'd better stay put and find out what this guy is up to. The stranger could be scouting the layout of the place for a future heist. Rustlers weren't limited to the old West. The elder Cross stooped below the crest of the hill and observed as the driver stood motionless, the binoculars fixed to his eyes. *What is he focused on so intently?* Jeff's eyes followed the man's line of vision. *Good God, his son and Ariel stepped off the cottage's well-lit porch in perfect view. Which one of the two was the interloper spying on? It didn't matter. Either way, the man's sneaky actions marked him as nefarious* and *his intentions registered as much more sinister than rustling horses.* Half sliding, half hurdling down the sharp incline, Jeff hurried back to the house, intent on warning Gavin and Ariel.

Chapter 16

Ariel squeezed toothpaste onto the bristles of her blue toothbrush. She gazed in the bathroom mirror of the farm cottage as she started the up and down motion across her straight white teeth. With Gavin keeping her company in the barn tonight, she relished the routine work even more and enjoyed a new found sense of security. There was no niggling dread of a certain ex-boyfriend showing up to beat the snot out of her. Weird, but she didn't realize the fear of his return was so insidious. She had sunk the worry far into the recesses of her mind. Otherwise it would incapacitate her. A restraining order meant nothing to Drake Porter, so she'd escaped to Wildwood Farms, where she remained hidden in plain sight from his abuse. The incident at Eight Seconds bar was a warning to Drake. He was no match for Gavin. She retained certainty; whatever his desires were for her didn't include his own death wish.

Her guard was down in more ways than one. Had she actually invited a military man into her bed and into her heart?

Ariel could see him in the bedroom behind her getting undressed with only his t-shirt left to shed. She appreciated the glorious view and the man. No previous partner caused her to laugh as much as Gavin. Who would have believed a bona-fide counter-terrorist nicknamed 'Caveman' could have such an edgy, brilliant wit? "Not me, but yes, he does." She spat out foam with the answer to her own question.

Gavin responded, swaggering into the bathroom. "Yes, already? I haven't even told you what I have in store for you tonight." Wrapping his arms around her waist from behind, he kissed her neck in soft, little pecks while turning her to face him. Without shifting his gaze from her face, he took the toothbrush out of her hand and put it on the counter. He grabbed a hand towel and gingerly dabbed the remaining toothpaste from the corners of her lips. Peering at her naked breasts he delicately swished the soft cotton around each areola. Her nipples perked and stiffened in response.

"For all your toughness and bravado, you're actually sweet, Mr. Navy man." She simmered, rubbing her pelvis into his body. She closed her eyes, pursed her lips, and tossed her head back, inviting him to kiss her.

Without hesitation, Gavin gently wrapped her dangling hair around his wrist, keeping her head back and answered the beckon of Ariel's full puckered lips. "I'll show you sweet, woman."

She whimpered as her mouth parted for a taste of his tongue and smelled peppermint before she sampled it. "Umm. Spicy. Just like you." Her tongue darted deeper for a more thorough examination of the exquisite flavor. He directed his response coursing in and out of her mouth in a slow winding dance. She moaned and gyrated into his stiffening groin, moving in a semi-circle back and forth.

He stepped back, a salacious grin on his face. "Time for bed, young lady." His tone smoldered as he deftly hoisted her in his arms, his heart thumping visibly against his ribs and strode toward the bedroom.

With a wanton haste, Gavin deposited Ariel on the bed and quickly stripped off his only remaining article of clothing.

Naked and erect, he eyed Ariel's bikinis and with mission proficiency, yanked them down her legs and tossed them on the floor next to his underwear.

He dove onto the bed next to her accessing the magic between her legs with his tongue.

Ariel fisted his hair in her hands and whimpered, "Oh G, it feels so good. You're torturing me. I want you inside, now."

Gavin extended one final lick and flipped on his back. He opened the drawer of the bedside table, retrieving the foil package he stored there earlier. Sliding the contents on in one smooth roll, he shifted on top of Ariel's writhing body probing his way to her entrance. "Oh, baby, you're so very ready." He grunted, moaned and thrust hard, his blue eyes serious and dark with heat.

She sensed his need and thrust her hips toward him pumping in and out. With each stroke her desire turned more primal. Oblivious to everything around her, she groaned and tossed her head, giving in to the thrill of sensation spreading swiftly from her feminine core to every inch of her body. She held tight to Gavin's massive arms as her body sagged, sated and limp. Her mind turned numb cancelling any doubts she could deliver and enjoy wild monkey sex with Mr. HOOYA himself.

Gavin's face scrunched up, "Baby, you good? Cause I'm fighting to prevent the inevitable explosion of pleasure heading south."

"Really good," she purred, as she wrapped her legs

around his waist, aware the self-discipline he prided himself in, crumbled.

He held Ariel's bottom tight to his crotch as he grunted in ecstasy, "AHHHHH." He pumped a few more times before he lay still on top of her. "God, I've never had sex this intense. You always amaze me, doctor," he said as he smoothed her tousled hair, tucking the errant strands on her face behind her ears and licking the drops of sweat as they trickled down her flushed cheek.

"Likewise," she responded.

****

Sex was the best sleep aid ever invented, Ariel mused as Gavin drifted off in a peaceful slumber beside her, assisted by a light snore and a half smile. She plumped the pillows behind her and unfolded the covers enough to slip between the cool cotton sheets. Her eyelids drooped, heavy from need of sleep, but she decided to read a few pages in the hard-to-put-down political thriller she started last weekend. Sierra recommended it as a two thumbs up read and she was right, as usual. The clock's digital screen displayed eleven thirty in blue. She decided to read until the witching hour.

Her first appointment tomorrow was booked for ten. She would have ample time if she woke up at eight and somehow eluded distractions from sleeping beauty.

She delved deeper into the plot, the pages whipped by as the intrigue intensified. Gavin stirred next to her, rolling over on his side. Ariel scanned the words, her focus so glued to the page she didn't notice her bedmate until his leg twitched. She glanced over and noticed his forehead covered in beads of feverous sweat and his eyelids fluttering in a frenetic wave.

The blunt force of a blind kick connected with her thigh sending extreme pain radiating down her leg. The doctor's quick reflexes enabled her to catch her fall as she rolled off the bed and landed on all fours. Agony best described Ariel's first attempt to stand but the immediate danger overrode physical considerations. Panicked, she limped to the armchair where he tossed his clothes before bed. She blindly searched under the stack until she made contact with the cold metal of his gun. They had made a mutual agreement earlier in the day to let him keep his firearm in the room but only if unloaded. She couldn't be sure Gavin ever delivered on the promise. He was too busy delivering on another promise. With the weapon in her hand, she pressed the magazine release button and it clattered to the floor, empty. *He's a man of his word. Thank God.* As she bent to retrieve the magazine, Gavin shouted a phrase in a language she'd never heard.

Now what? Do I wake him up and take the chance he'll deck me, or worse? She witnessed his arms flailing and swinging but he remained in bed, so she made a decision, hoping it was the correct one. Ariel stayed in her current position near the bedroom door and gently called his name, "Gavin, Gavin honey, wake up. You're having a bad dream, baby."

His glazed-over eyes opened, still under the influence of some horrible memory and distorted reality. Determined to nudge him gently back, she continued, "Gavin, listen to my voice. You're safe. I'm right here…for you." He mumbled another, what sounded like Arabic phrase, followed by a guttural command and a sweeping right hook. Good thing he'd knocked her out of bed, she grimaced as she touched her thigh. *It's time for my secret weapon.*

She stepped back to open the door and let Wager enter the room. He rushed in, wagged his tail, and whimpered. As if the canine understood his role, he let out a yelp like the one he gave Gavin after receiving a treat, leapt on the bed and licked his owner's face from chin to hairline. The dog bounced from side to side, seemingly alert to the possibility of lethal arms in motion. Lick, bounce, lick, bounce, like a game of wrestle the giant, Wager sprung over his prone-positioned owner until Gavin sat upright. Puzzled but amused, he eyed the attentive dog leap-frogging over him and patted his thigh. Wager yipped and sprawled unafraid on the familiar lap of his beloved master.

Gavin rubbed the border collie's multi-colored ears and addressed Ariel, keeping his attention on Wager, "I had an episode, didn't I?"

She guessed the hard-charging man didn't look at her because he was embarrassed so she sought to ease his discomfort with humor. "Yes, a straight-up nightmare. You even spoke in a foreign tongue." She noticed him wince. He scratched Wager behind the ears.

"Did I, um, hurt you?" He scrutinized her face for possible confirmation.

She didn't hesitate or flinch. "Nope. Like I said, you had an old fashioned nightmare, with a lot of incomprehensible garble, but you never left the bed."

His shoulders relaxed and his brow eased. "Whew. My first sleep over, but I didn't pee the bed or break anything. Maybe she'll invite me over again." He winked and offered his beautiful, infectious smile.

"Hey, since when did the furry beast get to sleep in your house?"

She frowned and he immediately picked up on it. "Note to self, don't call dog a hair missile or a furry beast in vet's presence." He patted the bed, an encouragement for her to join him. "What are you doing way over there?"

Ariel, prompted by the intense throbbing from her left thigh, walked in an exaggerated model step, foot over foot, toward the bed. Conscious the fake gait was a poor attempt at masking the injury from his keen eye, she unbuttoned her nightshirt and let the opening slide flirtatiously over her shoulder. "For your information, Wager has been sleeping with me since I arrived at Wildwood and only abandoned me when you acted out. He's great protection and a reassuring companion, if you catch my drift."

"Oh, I caught it all right," his eyes glued to her bare shoulder. "However, the real issue is your ex. He's a real piece of work, Ariel, but I have no intention of letting him anywhere near you. Between Wager and me you'll be safe, my guarantee and my promise."

Chapter 17

The rest of the night was episode free to Gavin's relief. Or at least he assumed so; based on the fact he woke up spooning with Ariel who was spooning with Wager. One incident a night was plenty for him but the fact he hadn't donned his battle gear and gone roving seemed like a positive sign.

Naked was the way he preferred her, without covers hauled up to her chin. He eyed the nightshirt on the floor where he'd tossed it last night. Inspired by the memory, he ripped the sheet back in lustful desire and wanton appreciation of her toned body. The morning sun poured through the bedroom window and illuminated her light olive skin. How did he get so lucky? She was everything he'd ever fantasized about. He lifted his hand to stroke her long leg and froze mid-air. What the hell? A substantial purple and slightly swollen circle marked her thigh. Aware she didn't have any birthmarks except the perfect dark mole on her back, which she flippantly referred to as a beauty mark, what the holy crap was this? Did an uncooperative patient kick her?

The doctor's job was very physical, one where even a sharp knock against a stall corner created a nasty mark. She currently supervised live mount breeding and a robust stallion primed to have his way with a willing mare represented more danger than any number of sea creatures he'd encountered.

Funny. He didn't remember seeing the bruise last night and he examined every inch of her luscious body, up close and personal. His mind filled with dread as a shocking realization dawned on him…a fresh bruise, deep blue and black showed up this morning after he'd been in her bed. He didn't want to admit the obvious but he'd most likely inflicted harm on her during his nightmare. His empty stomach wretched as acidic bile churned up his throat making him dry-heave. He gulped for air as panic and despair gripped his heart. He fucking hurt her. Self-loathing rode his mental state. She was obviously too afraid to actually trust him with the truth, so she lied. Didn't she realize the danger she put herself in by not telling him? Heat raced up his neck and face as he tamped down the anger. He was responsible for the damage to her but his actions were about to get checked. He slid to the edge of the bed; eyes steady on Ariel, rose to his feet and tip toed to the chair where he'd left his clothes. Wager raised his head and regarded his owner, thumping his tail on the mattress. Gavin placed his index finger to his lips in a motion for silence, grabbed his shoes, tucked the heap of clothes under his arm, and slipped out the door.

****

Careful not to let the screen slam shut, Gavin eased the door back into its frame. He hopped alternately on one foot tugging his pants on, and then slid his sneakers over the arches of his feet as he fumbled off the porch. The truth hurt but Ariel lacked the trust to confide in him. He'd planted the bruise on her thigh. He didn't doubt she loved him but without unconditional trust a long-term relationship couldn't be nurtured, much less exist. Theirs would sizzle hot and burn out like a Fourth of July sparkler. Enough dicking around. Time to act. There was too much riding on this decision. He'd seek help at the Naval Hospital Jacksonville.

"Where's the fire, son?" Jeff asked, a curious look on his face.

Not one to be easily startled, Gavin dropped the remaining bundle of clothes and jerked to a stop in front of his amused father. His mind spun searching for excuses, reasons why, and smart ass comebacks. Nothing. He was a mental blank and caught red-handed, sneaking out of his girlfriend's house.

"Oh, hi Dad. I didn't see you there," he said, his tone nonchalant.

"Yeah," Jeff noted. "So it appears." He smiled approvingly and clapped his son on the shoulder. "We need to talk. Something or I should say someone, has come up. Walk with me." He pointed to the barn and away from Ariel's cottage.

Gavin shifted his simmering petulance to neutral, shoved his hands in his pockets and in step with his Dad ambled across the gravel drive. "I'm listening."

Jeff relayed the bizarre scene he'd witnessed in the back pasture. "I'm hoping to flush out any data you might have and put it together with mine."

Gavin's aloof expression shifted into a scowl. "I do have information, Dad."

Jeff nodded and continued, "Do you think he's a rustler?"

Gavin wasted no time with his answer. "No, I don't. He's worse than a horse thief. He's a woman beater and a disgusting excuse for a human being, much less a man."

Jeff inhaled sharply and grabbed Gavin's arm. "The man's after Dr. Armstrong? Do you know him?"

Gavin perceived the alarm on his father's face and tempered his explanation with sarcasm, "Well, I wouldn't exactly call us friends. I had an altercation with the scum bag in a bar parking lot the other night when I caught him keying Ariel's truck."

Jeff faced Gavin. "What the hell, son?" The pitch of his voice rose to tenor. "You didn't think it was important to tell me?"

Gavin sensed his father's frustration and regretted not telling him sooner. "Sorry Dad. I honestly didn't want to burden you with some narcissistic asshole's juvenile prank. Besides, the sheriff took him into custody for violating his restraining order. I honestly didn't think he'd be a problem but he must have posted bail."

"That's your rationale? You didn't want to burden me?" Jeff's temper flared.

"Okay, okay. Ariel didn't want you to find out. Having made such a terrible choice embarrassed her and she worried you'd think less of her or hold it against her. Maybe not hire her."

"Son, you know me better than anyone and so should she, by now. I wouldn't dream of laying the responsibility for his insanity on her. Besides, she's one of us now and deserves our protection. This is serious if a restraining order has been issued. Stalking is no joke and he's gone to the trouble of tracking her down. There's no telling what he'll do. We need to call the sheriff."

Gavin frowned. He realized his father's assessment of the potential danger to both the woman he loved and his family's farm was spot on. "He's apparently ignored the law but we'll have to prove he violated the order before we call the sheriff and have him picked up."

Jeff searched Gavin's face. "One thing's for sure. We need to come up with a plan and fast. I recommend we involve Rob. He works with her daily making the rounds and we can count on his discretion."

"Good idea. We'll read him in as soon as he arrives to start his shift." He slowly rubbed his chin. "We can definitely lock this place down but how do we protect Ariel when she leaves the farm? She's way too independent to allow anyone body guarding her."

"Well son, we're going to find out how good you are working surveillance and keeping secrets from someone you're sleeping with," he said, raising an eyebrow. "I advise no pillow talk."

Gavin dragged a hand through his hair. He couldn't guarantee what he'd do or wouldn't do sharing a bed with Ariel. The struggle wasn't solely about him anymore. Her life depended on him getting back to battery and fast.

Chapter 18

"Not a word of this to Ariel." Jeff cautioned his two co-conspirators. "There's no need to alarm her."

Gavin spoke up, "Agreed. We need to build a protective perimeter around Dr. Armstrong with one of us in close proximity to her at all times."

Rob, the farm manager, replied, "My work with her is mostly here in the barn holding the horses while she does treatments and exams. So anytime she's making rounds in the barn, I've got her covered."

Jeff nodded. "Good. Then, it'll seem routine to her." He leaned in, a serious mien clouding his face. "Listen, her ex-boyfriend is dangerous. Stay alert. I don't know when or what his next crazy-assed move might be."

"Boss," he pointed to the narrow corner outside the tack room, "I have a pitchfork handy and a sharp knife right here." He patted his hip and folded back the corner of his shirt to reveal a long, curved blade in a leather scabbard hooked to his belt.

"The blade seems lethal and I suspect if threatened, you're capable of defending yourself, but don't be a hero." His voice dropped, "She'll be out shortly to do her rounds. When she finishes, text me and I'll take over. My watch is going to require a bit of finesse and a small amount of trickery as I usually meet with her first thing in the morning and disappear."

"Will do," Rob replied.

Jeff, still speaking to Rob, gazed at his son. "If we can cover her during the day, I think Gavin prefers night watch." He gave his son an inconspicuous wink.

"I'm leaving now," Gavin stated without animation. He gave Rob a firm handshake and disappeared out the back, calling over his shoulder, "Appointment in Jacksonville. Be back in a few hours."

Rob chuckled at the innuendo. "Well, heads up Boss. She usually drives the golf cart out to the back pasture once a day to observe the mares and their babies while she eats her lunch. She usually goes alone."

"What are you two conspiring about?" Ariel joked as she sauntered into the barn, coffee in one hand and bridle in the other. It amused her when the two men's heads jerked up in unison at the sound of her voice. Their eyes grew wide and mouths hung open like two little boys caught with a hand in the cookie jar.

Jeff's attention jumped to the bridle. "Are you going for a ride?"

"Yeah, right after I do the morning treatments I planned to ride one of the geldings out to the back pasture instead of driving the golf cart. It's such a glorious day. Last night's thunder storm really dropped the humidity. Wouldn't you agree?"

Jeff exchanged a knowing glance with Rob. "You want some company?"

"Sure, but I didn't realize you did much riding."

Rob piped in. "Oh, the boss is a real cowboy."

"Well, the business of the farm keeps me busy most of the time but I do enjoy an occasional gallop across the fields. And as you mentioned it is another perfect summer day. I'll fetch my gear while you do the rounds." Jeff did a quick about face and disappeared out of the barn into the bright Florida sunshine.

"Is everything okay with Jeff?" Ariel's brows drew together. "He seemed...I don't know, uncomfortable? And what's with the Mick Dundee knife, Rob?"

Rob occupied his hands with a halter and a lead rope turning his back to Ariel hiding the 'oh shit' slipping from his mouth. "Bobcats."

"Bobcats, what?" she questioned. "You've seen bobcats on the farm?"

"Yeah, Jeff found a new born calf with tell-tale claw marks, mauled and gutted in the back field near where the highway runs along the property. We're not taking any chances and neither should you." He met her eyes with intensity.

"I'll keep my third eye open," she snorted, too light hearted to worry about an elusive creature who primarily hunted at night and used his almost supernatural sense of smell to avoid all human contact.

"In the meantime we should get started so when Cowboy Jeff comes back the treatments are completed." Ariel cocked an eyebrow at Rob while she lifted the first chart off the door of her favorite filly. Nike's upper lip nibbled the hair on the top of her head in a familiar welcome. When the doctor didn't raise her eyes from the chart, the precocious two year old struck the stall door with her front hoof and squealed. "You big spoiled baby," Ariel chided the filly while she rubbed the soft nose jutted into her outstretched hand. "You need a spanking." She grinned as she took the offered halter from Rob who, Ariel observed, stood at a cautious distance to complete the hand off. Nike responded to the half-hearted threat with an immediate toss of her head followed by a nicker. Ariel unbolted the latch, stepped into the stall, and placed the halter over the horse's lowered head. Rob walked forward to hold the lead while Ariel massaged down Nike's legs and checked for swelling.

All the fillies play together on a regular basis with Nike usually dominating the field but yesterday one of the other fillies gave as good as she got and landed a sideways kick on Nike's leg. Placed correctly it could have been a career ender but the ever-alert-goddess-of-speed dodged the full blow and merely got nicked. Jeff would be happy to hear there was no swelling on his prized horse. She appeared ready for another round in the back pasture filly bowl.

"Doc, how's it look?"

"We dodged a bullet, Rob. The little lady has a small cut on her leg but no bruising or swelling.

"Let's see her gait. Trot her down and back on her lead rope. Go on the other side of the stalls so I can observe her in the sunlight."

Ariel observed as Rob led her out of the stall, out into the sunshine, and broke her into a trot. The vet breathed a sigh of relief as the horse moved forward with effortless grace. Rob halted in front of Ariel who swept her hand up under Nike's mane and rewarded her sound performance with steady firm pats.

"I know it's hard, girl, but behave." Her accent heavy on the first syllable of the last word, she gave a final slap on Nike's neck as Rob led her back into her stall.

"While you secure our resident princess, I'll check out the new brood mare in the next barn and then saddle up the horses," Ariel informed Rob and scooted out the door before he could stop her.

She checked all the vitals of a recently purchased mare and noted the routine findings on the chart before Rob caught up with her.

"Dr. Armstrong. How about waiting for me next time?" She noticed he seemed perturbed because he called her by her professional name. But then Rob was way too serious most of the time.

"What happened? Did Nike give you some attitude without me there to supervise?"

"No, she was a perfect angel," he said, his voice edged with sarcasm. "We don't know anything about the new mare and you shouldn't examine her alone in an empty barn." His tone changed to exasperation.

Surprise blossomed on Ariel's face. "Uh, Rob I'm a veterinarian and board certified in reproduction. I think I know my way around a brood mare and a stable for sure. What's gotten into you?"

"Forget it, Doc. I guess the bobcat presence spooked me. Until he's caught, I'd like to stay close if it's okay with you. Indulge me, please."

"Sure thing, Mr. Worry Wart." Puzzled by his behavior but willing to comply she pointed to the tack room. "How about fetching Jeff's gear and let's get the horses saddled up."

She worked with Rob in silence without their usual banter as she struggled to make sense of his strange behavior. She doubted whatever motivated his clinginess had a damn thing to do with bobcats. Rob grew up in the country and spent his youth navigating every corner of the local woods, hunting resident wildlife. Maybe Jeff had a clue and would be willing to share with her.

Ariel finished cinching the saddle, grabbed the reins of the gelding, and led him out to the front of the barn where Rob stood waiting with Jeff's mount.

Rob texted on his phone. "I'll let the boss know we're ready."

Within minutes, Jeff came barreling out the side door of the main house.

He wore an open carry pistol on his narrow hip. Her voice tilted up with curiosity, "You expecting trouble?"

"You never know when you might run into a rattlesnake hiding under a rock." His jaw constricted as he meted out the words.

"I thought it was bobcats?" She placed her foot in the stirrup, swung her right leg over the gelding's back, and settled in the saddle.

"Bobcats?" the older man questioned, hesitating for an instant, as he gripped the reins along with the saddle horn.

"Rob said you found a mauled calf in the upper meadow with claw marks."

"Uh-huh," Jeff nodded, keeping his gaze straight ahead as he eased into the saddle of his blood bay horse.

Ariel took note of Jeff's brief and under the circumstances, odd reply but decided to let it ride for now. She squeezed her knees into Casanova's side and clucked, moving the horse forward at a trot. Good thing she wore jeans to work. The deep blue and black mark colored her leg like an angry storm and she was short on explanations. After slathering half the tube of pain cream on her bruised thigh, the relentless throbbing subsided and Ariel thanked the arnica gods for making such an effective salve. Kicking her was an accident. She could think of no good reason to tell Gavin and have him torture himself with guilt over something he did in his sleep.

Jeff trotted alongside Ariel for half a mile when he spontaneously signaled with a roll of his hand, the desire to nudge the horses into a canter. Without hesitating, she leaned forward and tapped the young gelding's flank sending him headlong down the dirt road at a heady speed. The landscape blurred. Tears whipped up by the wind slid down her face and laced her lips with a salty taste. The sound of pounding hoofs thundered louder. Jeff was gaining on them. An experienced equestrian, Ariel loosened the reins along the thoroughbred's sweaty neck and bent forward. His coarse black mane covered her face while his long, powerful strides swallowed the earth in a sweeping, fluid gallop.

The equine motto, in her mind, read something like, 'ask and you shall receive…everything I've got.' "C'mon Cass," she clucked, "let's win this race." As if he understood, the muscles in his hindquarters tightened under her and he surged forward. Exhilaration filled every cell of her body and her heart sang with happiness as the magnificent four-legged creature sprang ahead and sped around the final bend. The gate to the back pasture, the agreed upon finish line, loomed. Ariel tightened the reins, sat back in the saddle, and tilted her heels down. Cass responded and slowed to a trot, then smoothly receded to a springy walk and stopped in front of the gate. "We won," she giggled softly in his ear.

Jeff jumped down from his mount and unlatched

the gate, allowing Ariel and Cass to pass through. He followed on foot, leading his horse and closed the opening behind him. "Nice sprint, Doctor Armstrong."

"Thanks. Cass is all heart and intuition," she said, vigorously patting her mount's neck. "Horses rule." She fist-pumped in the air.

Ariel spotted a large oak with plenty of shade and pointed Cass's head toward the tree. "We can view the whole pasture from the top of the knoll." She nodded her head toward the century old oak dominating the hilltop landscape. "We'll have an unobstructed view of the mamas and their babies too."

"Perfect," Jeff said, his head swiveling back along the fence line, surveying for evidence of the watcher. "Let's grab a bite to eat and watch the show."

Ariel bit into her chicken salad sandwich and chewed. "Ummm. Bessie Mae has outdone herself once again. My blue jeans are getting tight from all the fresh, home-made food." She raised her right index finger to the corner of her lip and slid an escaped morsel into her mouth.

"Yeah. You and me both, kiddo, but I don't think you're in danger of needing bigger pants with all the physical work you do here."

He smiled at the doctor as he tapped his side to make sure the gun was still holstered to his side.

"Jeff, is there something you want to tell me?" she inquired, her brown eyes focused and penetrating.

"What do you mean?"

"Well, Rob is hovering like a quarterback with a fumbled football, walking around with his super sharp, scary knife. When I questioned him about it he got pissy and claimed you found evidence of a bobcat out on the farm's perimeter. I continued to the main barn pursuing my usual rounds and he acted annoyed when I left him behind. Then, you appear with a fully loaded pistol lodged on your hip and state rattlesnakes have taken over the neighborhood. So, level with me, what's really going on?"

"I assure you the vermin around here are nothing to worry your head about, my dear doctor. Remember, Wager tangled with a fanged critter and we do get the occasional wild animal lurking around. Some precautions are warranted. Wouldn't you agree?"

"What about Rob?"

"Rob is just being Rob and truthfully he's had SEAL envy ever since he started working here and hanging out with Gavin. So, you care for the domesticated animals and we'll see to anything else. Deal?"

"Deal," she agreed with him but she wasn't convinced. Somehow her gut told her she wasn't getting the full story. Maybe he'd be more forthcoming about Gavin's whereabouts.

"Hey, speaking of Gavin, where is he today? I woke up this morning and he was gone." Her breath sucked back on the final three words but the bag was wide open and the cat was running free. Heat rose up her face. Well, if Jeff wasn't aware she was sleeping with his son before, he was now.

Jeff replied, "Gavin apparently had an epiphany and drove to the Naval Hospital Jacksonville to chat with a doctor who specializes in PTSD. Evidently Ariel, you had a lot to do with his decision."

****

Gavin waited, his right knee bobbing up and down

to match the unrelenting pounding of his heart. He checked his watch, again. Five minutes later than the last time he looked. He checked the number on the closed door. Room 225. Yep, he was in the correct waiting area. *What's taking so friggin' long? The doc said he'd fit me in but how busy could he be this early in the morning?* He squirmed in his chair as he recalled his brief conversation with the man. The good doctor was not a shrink as he first thought but a neurologist. Dr. Romero was quick to make the distinction and acted like he was expecting Gavin to call. *Kudos to Tony and the Chief for non-shrink recommendation.*

The door swung open. Gavin stood, expecting the man whose focus was instantly on him to announce, "I'm ready for the next head case." Instead he walked over, hand extended, smiling, casual. "Gavin?"

"Yeah." He met the doctor's firm grip with one of his own.

"Nice to meet you. Let's go in my office." He assumed a relaxed stance indicating the direction, letting Gavin take the lead into his office.

The décor was Navy all the way and not as stuffy as he had pictured. The maritime wall clock quietly ticked as he studied the filled bookshelf stacked with science fiction, political intrigue and noticeably absent of medical diagnosis books. Gavin observed Dr. Romero remained standing in the center of the room, hands in his pockets, quiet, while Gavin continued his perusal of the interior. Satisfied he would be comfortable in the surroundings, he faced the doctor and had the urge to give him a high five and a "HOOYAH" but instead took a seat in a leather chair with his back to the wall.

Dr. Romero took a seat opposite Gavin. "Do you want to remain on the Teams?" he asked flatly.

Thankfully, spared from typical small talk but surprised by the bluntness of the question, Gavin hesitated, gripping the sides of the chair, he spit out, "Are you fucking kidding me? Yes."

"Glad to hear so. I've already reviewed your file and it's clear you're a skilled operator with a stellar service record who's been sent out on an ungodly number of dangerous missions."

"Sums it up."

"Let's get started, then. Before I refer you to the shrink I'm ordering a cat scan and a complete physical."

"Why?"

"Didn't an IED detonate, blow you off a Humvee on to your hard head, and give you a concussion?"

"Yeah, but…"

"No buts Petty Officer. I want to rule out traumatic brain injury, also known as TBI, before we go the PTSD route. With a diagnosis of post-traumatic stress it could be months before you go back to the Teams, if ever."

Gavin's eyes shifted toward the ceiling recalling a mental image of the deep bruise on Ariel's thigh. "There's something you need to know. It's not in the medical report but it's the only reason I'm here."

Dr. Romero nodded, "Go ahead."

"The other night I was sleeping with…someone and I had a nightmare, a violent nightmare." His voice cracked. "I hurt her, doc."

"I see. What do you remember?"

"I was reliving the day in Afghanistan when my

team was patrolling with Marine Recon. I was serving as point man but I didn't see the mound of dirt from the IED. It's my fault the young Marine Lieutenant got injured and the other Marine who was driving, got killed. The Humvee landed on top of the kid and now he's paralyzed."

"The report I read stated you saved his life, as well as several other Marines. If you hadn't eliminated the Taliban sniper they'd all be dead."

"I'm sure the Lieutenant is grateful to me for his future in a wheel chair," he countered, his voice tinged with icy contempt.

Dr. Romero changed the subject, "What's the extent of your female friend's injuries?"

"I kicked her in the leg, her thigh to be exact. She didn't say anything about the bruise but I think it's because she's afraid of me."

"Why do you think she's afraid of you?"

"Because, when I asked her what happened, she lied to me and claimed I had a "normal" nightmare."

"I understand."

"Do you?" He glared. "Because this can't ever happen again, Doc." His fist slammed the chair's armrest.

Dr. Romero gazed calmly at Gavin. "The first thing we need to do is ensure you get a restful sleep without night terrors."

"What are you going to do, shoot me?" he asked, his tone caustic.

Continuing his cool demeanor, the doctor responded, "No, I'm prescribing a sleep aid for you. It calms nocturnal brain activity and blocks specific pathways so you won't sleep walk."

"Oh, zombie meds. Sure, whatever." He resigned himself to taking the meds the doctor prescribed.

"I'm not a psychiatrist Gavin, I'm a neurologist and if you have a traumatic brain injury the drug will help regulate your brain activity. I assume you care about this woman so work with me and take the meds until we can sort out a diagnosis or don't sleep with her."

Well, no way the latter was going to happen. He extended his palm for the prescription.

Chapter 19

The first rays of morning peeked through the white plantation blinds in Ariel's bedroom. She stretched her arms above her head, and pondered the exquisite joy of being alive. Gavin's light snore woke her but it didn't matter because the deep up and down rhythm of his chest indicated a sound sleep. Only a week after his initial visit with Dr. Romero and the tough SEAL was baby snoozing against her, curled in a fetal position, mouth half-opened. The medication was working. *Thank God.*

He lifted one eye lid. "Where're you going?"

"I thought you were asleep?"

"I was but I woke up when you tried to sneak out of bed," he joked.

"Busy day ahead for those of us who work for a living," she teased, perched on the edge of the bed, combing her fingers through her hair.

"Don't get sassy with me, woman. You're going to be late for work today," he growled, flipping her on top of him. Her long waves of thick hair billowed in his face as he wrapped his arms around her waist and skimmed her neck with sweet, light kisses, emphasizing his need.

She giggled as she pretended to struggle against his powerful hold. "Let me go, you big bully. I…"

He planted a lingering kiss on her lips and

murmured, "Nice, fresh floral scent." His hand found its way down her narrow hip to the pale purple splotch remaining on her thigh and circled it with his index finger. "Did you think I wouldn't figure out how you got the bruise?"

"You had enough weighing you down without me adding more shit to the scale."

"You should have told me. Remember your sermon about trust?"

"Sermon?" Incredulous, she straightened her arms and arched her back, hovering above him. "I'm a vet, not a preacher and it was a talk."

"Well, the *talk*," he responded, his fingers in quote marks, "sounded a tad preachy, Doctor Armstrong, but the point is we shouldn't have secrets going forward. Agreed?"

She wasn't sure what he meant by 'going forward' but she nodded in agreement.

He grabbed a fist full of caramel-colored hair draping Ariel's naked shoulder and tugged until her face was inches from his. "I love you, Ariel."

And there it was, the going forward fully defined. She couldn't deny she loved him too, so much, she ached but rather than return the sentiment she captured his mouth with her tongue, blissfully tasting him. Tugging his shoulders, she rolled, reversing their position. Ariel raised her hips in a wanton search for his erection and Gavin complied directing his manhood into the apex between her hips. Her desire spiraled into lust and filled with her ecstasy. She moaned and sank her nails into his back as she tumbled over the divine edge. He followed closely behind with his own release and filled her with his passion.

He rested quietly on top of her for a minute before lifting his body so he was braced over her. "Now you can go to work, baby." He kissed her flushed cheek.

"Well, now, I don't want to." She arched up and inhaled his musky sex scent, giving him a quick lip smack.

She should tell him about the job offer she'd received right now while the mood was tranquil. They had agreed to be honest with each other but after he professed his love to her she was conflicted. Was it possible to have a future with Gavin thousands of miles from home? She assumed he'd receive a medical release in a few weeks and return to active duty. She'd continue at Wildwood farms, reminded every day of what transpired between them, preoccupied with hoping he'd make it back alive. Could she live with the worry? Could she deal with the dread every time someone knocked on the door or the phone rang in the middle of the night? Was it possible to live without him in her bed? For now, she'd keep her secret. She still had time to make a decision. The job wasn't available for a couple of months. Those months would give her time to see how John adapted to farm life.

"You seem preoccupied. Is everything okay? Or maybe I should ask *was* everything okay?"

"You're kidding, right?"

His turquoise eyes penetrated her soul and she wondered if he could read her thoughts, "Everything is…you are…we're so tuned in, it's perfect G." She smoothly rolled out from under him and off the bed and with a back glance, offered a sweet smile, "But I have to show up for work sometime today."

He nodded his head toward the shower and gave

her a shit-eating grin. "You have to shower, don't you?"

"You're insatiable." She grabbed her clothes off the chair and sprinted for the bathroom, slamming the door and clicking the lock as Gavin grabbed for the outside handle. "Wait your turn, Mr. SEAL." She giggled as he jiggled the doorknob. With her ear placed against the wood, she listened. Silence. Turning on the water she glanced at the door before stepping behind the shower curtain. She assumed he sauntered downstairs to fix coffee but her intuition screamed, 'He's up to something.' Ignoring her instincts, she delved into deep reverie about the future, weighing all angles of the looming decision. She poured a small amount of shampoo in her hair and closed her eyes as she massaged her scalp. A cool draft of air chilled her skin. She winked one eye open as the curtain slid forward. "I passed..." registered, before she let loose an ear-splitting scream. She pivoted to see Gavin holding the edge of the curtain, a boyish grin on his face. He waved a credit card at her.

"A fun fact you didn't know about me. I passed the lock picking class with flying colors." He raised his arm just in time to ward off the bar of soap flying toward his head.

"Dinner tonight?" he asked as he backed out of the bathroom, the look of an errant teenager on his face.

She stuck her soap-covered head around the corner of the curtain. "Yeah, I have to go to the Naval Hospital today but I'll be back in time to get even with you."

"I can't wait." He backed up a few steps, pausing a safe distance away. "What time are you planning to arrive in Jacksonville?"

She ducked her head back in the shower seeking the running water in front of her. "This afternoon as soon as I finish my rounds."

"Seeing your brother?"

"Yeah, and checking with his doctor to find out his release date so I can move him here, to the farm." She turned the water off, grabbed a towel and wrapped it around her head, turban style.

"I have an appointment with my doctor this afternoon to get my cat scan. We could drive together. I'd like to meet your brother."

"You would, would you?" she questioned, in a noncommittal tone. She stepped out of the shower, naked except for the towel wrapped around her head.

"Yeah and any excuse to be with you," he responded, gazing at her suntanned curves with apparent and unashamed desire.

"Behave." She pointed at his crotch. "Your growing interest in me isn't going unnoticed."

"Mr. Friendly has a mind of his own and a harder will, where you're concerned," Gavin murmured and stepped forward, his gaze smoldering.

Ariel raised her hand, palm out. "And hold on there, big boy. Baby needs a break. I have rounds to do."

"Check," he said, resigned.

"I can't always predict my schedule or when my rounds on the farm will be done but you have a definite appointment so why don't we meet there? I'll drive down as soon as I finish."

"Text me when you leave the farm and when you arrive at the hospital. I'll meet you at Starbucks. Coffee's on me. Oh, and carry your gun with you in the truck, okay?"

Ariel touched her fingers to his as she brushed by him on the way out the door. She briefly turned blowing him a kiss. She had no doubt the image of him standing naked and ripped in her bedroom would stay stuck in her mind all day like a song spinning around in your head over and over.

****

Gavin arrived five minutes early for his appointment with Dr. Romero. He intended to take care of business and head for the coffee shop downstairs so he didn't miss Ariel. The image of her lips puckered around a coffee cup caused an immediate bulge in his pants but despite his physical reaction, he had a more important motive for the coffee date. He decided to take a different tact for obtaining information about her injured brother by meeting her in an environment where she couldn't escape into veterinary duties. An environment where, because of her proximity to her brother, she was primed to discuss the situation. At the farm, she closed down every time he engaged her in a discussion about her brother's accident. He could have gone around her and found out any details he wanted but then there wouldn't be trust. She had been instrumental in his healing and now he sought to return the favor. He wanted her to trust him enough to share the grief she obviously experienced every time she visited the Naval Hospital in Jacksonville. He noted how the doctor always appeared stoic when she mentioned her brother but the deep sadness in her eyes gave away her mental suffering. It killed him to watch her bite her lower lip in an attempt to mask the quivering. And then there was the matter of the stalking ex-boyfriend and the need to keep a watchful eye out for Drake the Dick Head. Keeping her under his watchful eye was proving difficult. She was hard headed and too damned independent. To his relief there wasn't much opportunity for the little shit to try something in broad daylight on I-75 between the farm and the hospital. Still, he worried.

"Gavin, we're ready for you," Dr. Romero said opening the door to the exam room where the CAT scan was located.

Gavin straightened, instinctively grabbing the two loose ends of his hospital gown, and strode over to the equipment-laden bed. Assisted by a male nurse he positioned himself on his back. As the machine rolled in a steady hum above his upper body and over his head, he vowed silently to persist until he broke down all Dr. Armstrong's barriers. A brief detour back to Afghanistan might sidetrack him but he was in the relationship for the long haul. He'd finish his tour and be home to support her in her brother's recovery and her own healing. Somewhere along the line he'd made the crucial decision. Ariel was more important to him than being a Spec Ops operator. The loud whoosh, whoosh, thump, thump humming of the machine stopped.

"All done," Dr. Romero said with a smile. "The radiologist and I will look at the images today and let you know the results probably tomorrow. How are the meds working?"

Gavin hopped off the bed, glad the procedure was over. "I'm sleeping through the night without incident."

"Good to hear. Any night time tussles?" he asked in a matter of fact tone.

"Define 'tussles'?"

"Busted for being politically correct. Night terrors? Kicking, swinging…"

"Nope, not aware of any."

"I'm encouraged, Petty Officer. Let's get these test results and talk again tomorrow."

"Okay Doc. I'm headed over to SOCOM to talk to the Senior Chief." *But first I'm going downstairs to meet my 'tussle partner.'* The mental image of his very sexy tussle partner made him smile.

After a quick trip down the elevator, Gavin waited in line at the popular coffee klatch.

"What drink can I make for you sir?" the barista chirped.

"A grande hot chocolate with whipped cream, no lid and a grande latte with one sweet and low. He smiled at the surprised reaction to his order. Nobody orders hot chocolate in the summer in Florida but then he wasn't nobody. He was part of an elite fighting force where three hundred hopefuls try out and only thirty make it. And no matter what professional path he chose after the SEAL Teams, he would always retain the credo of the frogman.

"Gavin, your drinks are up." The same chirpy barista handed him the two beverages.

He turned in time to see Ariel enter the ground floor café. She strolled seamlessly through the crowd, too busy waving in his direction to notice all eyes fixated on her. Unlike his technique of muscling through the other patrons to the ordering spot, like he'd gut a fish, the mostly male clientele parted effortlessly as she approached.

"Is one of those for me?" Ariel asked, eyes darting

back and forth between the two choices.

Gavin held up the latte.

Ignoring the offered coffee, Ariel chuckled, "You and only one other person in the world I know order hot chocolate, lots of whipped cream, and no lid, in the summer, for Pete's sake."

"Who besides me?" he asked casually, sinking his lips into the whipped cream and slurping the top layer into his mouth.

"My brother," she replied retrieving the coffee. With one hand resting against Gavin's muscular chest, Ariel licked the sweet topping layering his upper lip. In one long sweep upwards her tongue crossed his cheek, and then headed for his chin lapping up the delectable substance.

Surprised by her open display of affection, Gavin froze. His breathing hitched as her tongue made a sensuous glide over his chin. He met her gaze as she peered up through thick dark lashes and made her final brush across his bottom lip. "Jesus, Ariel, if you're trying to give me a hard-on right here and now, mission accomplished." He raised his eyebrows as his eyes drifted south.

Laughing so hard her chest bounced, she gestured toward the door. "Want to go meet the other summer hot chocolate drinker?"

"Just stand there and drink your coffee. I need a minute." He shuffled his legs in an attempt to reposition the family jewels.

Buzzzz. Buzzzzz. Ariel grabbed the vibrating cell phone clipped on her belt and stared at the number showing on its green face. "Ugh."

"What is it?"

"Equine Emergency at the University. I gotta go. Rain check on meeting my brother and dinner? It might be a late night, so don't wait up."

"Okay." *She can't go alone.* "Do you want me to come with you? I can postpone my trip to SOCOM."

"You're sweet, but no. This one's on me. The U.F. surgeons are letting me scrub in so I can add another case in preparation for my board exam in reproduction."

His grin faded. He started to argue, "Well, wouldn't it be better if I drove so you could nap on the way up and..."

"Don't start," she huffed as she pointed her finger at him. "You'd just have to sit in the waiting room for God knows how long while I'm elbow deep in horse guts doing surgery. If the surgery goes on longer than expected and it gets too late, I'll drop anchor at Sierra's house. Sorry G. I'll make it up to you." She winked and clipped her cell phone back on her belt as she hurried out the door.

Gavin called out, "You already have."

He gave her a head start and then made a direct path for the parking lot. The left turn signal on her truck was blinking as she eased out into traffic. Scanning the lot and surrounding area to make sure no one pursued her, Gavin followed at a discreet distance. *Maybe Drake gave up. Not likely. Good thing I confiscated Sierra's contact information off Ariel's phone.*

Chapter 20

Ariel swiped at the blood dripping off the end of her surgical glove. "Brutal," she acknowledged out loud as she checked her watch and read the time, eleven-ten p.m. Glad she'd made prearrangements with her best friend, Sierra, to stay the night. She ripped off her gloves and tossed them in the sharps container. Lifting her scrubs, she retrieved her cell phone out of her back jeans pocket and texted her acceptance to crash at Sierra's house five minutes from the university rather than drive back to Ocala. The close proximity would give her an opportunity to check on the pricey thoroughbred's recovery tomorrow morning before she drove back to Wildwood Farms. The surgery turned out to require removal of a large tumor in the mare's uterus but she survived the surgery and her prognosis appeared good. She peeled off her blood-crusted outer clothes while the technical support staff buzzed around the surgery room no doubt anxious to get home to their families.

Weary from the long day, Ariel tapped out the message, "Be there in 30 minutes," into her phone and hit send.

She called out to the staff, "Thanks guys. Great job. See you tomorrow," and swung through the operating room doors to the hospital exit. Fishing her car keys out of her purse, she positioned her ignition key point first as instructed in her self-defense class. Peeking through the rear door window, the parking lot appeared deserted. Granted the area was fenced and gated with a coded entry, but in the darkness of night the huge, mostly empty space loomed ominous. *Don't be paranoid,* she told herself as she shoved open the metal door, and jogged toward the only vehicle in the parking lot. Halfway across the empty space, headlights flooded her path as a car sped down the drive toward the front gate. Adrenaline poured through her bloodstream as panic overwhelmed her senses. Ariel sprinted for her truck, clicking the unlock button on the fob as she ran. She yanked the handle open, ready to fling herself through the door, when the song, "Mama's Broken Heart," blared in her ears. Sierra's BMW slid to a screeching halt directly outside the gate. The car radio, turned to defcon three, was playing her favorite song. Her tensed muscles relaxed. Ariel released a deep sigh and walked to the gate keypad, punching in the security code.

She hugged her exuberant friend through the car's open window. "Geez Sierra, you had me going. What are you doing here? The plan was for me to come to your house."

"Your boyfriend called and very nicely ordered me to pick you up." She stretched across the leather seats and opened the passenger side door. "Hop in, princess. Your carriage awaits."

"This is silly. I have to come back tomorrow to check on the horse."

"I don't have my first Zumba fitness class until ten in the morning and no way am I telling Gavin I didn't follow orders." *Or that I left you alone so Mr. Creepy could stalk you.*

"I'm fully capable of handling my own affairs but I admit it's lovely to have someone taking care of me for a change." She offered an affectionate smile. "I'm pooped and I have to admit, the taxi service is a nice touch, girlfriend."

"All this and coffee in the morning," Sierra chimed, twirling her index finger in the air.

Ariel slid down in her seat, closed her eyes, and drifted into a light doze. Exhaustion threatened to take her under but she fought the urge to sleep. She wanted to mentally revive today's meeting with Gavin at the hospital. She sighed at the delicious memory of the sweet cream taste on Gavin's lips. Her breath sucked in and out in short little gasps as she recalled the particular rosemary mint smell of his shampoo while nuzzling her nose in his hair. He demolished her defenses like an ancient wall crumbling under assault from the sun and the wind. She anticipated their time together whenever they were apart. Trust and spontaneity had replaced the carefulness and inhibitions she'd accumulated from past entanglements. She'd withheld telling him she loved him, even when he'd so sincerely told her, but she couldn't conceive life without him. Was she being true to herself? She believed she could be happy without accepting the dream offer of employment in Lexington…with Gavin in her life. What if he didn't make it back this time? Her stomach churned and turned queasy. *Nope, not going there.* She'd deal with the worst possible scenario, if and when the time came.

"Ariel, we're home."

Sierra's voice bounced her out of her dream and back to reality. "Ugh, sorry I fell asleep on you." She rubbed a hand across her face. "I'm wiped out after the surgery but a good night's sleep and I'll be back in the game."

"Well, your 'cat got the cream' smile revealed your enjoyment of a pleasant fantasy and I'd be willing to guess who was frolicking in the dream with you." She smirked. "Speaking of Mr. Dreamboat, text him and let him know the package arrived or the bird's in the nest or whatever SEAL lingo conveys you're safely home with me."

Ariel chuckled at her best friend's ever-present humor as she tapped letters into her phone and hit send. "Mission accomplished. I hope I didn't wake him up."

"He's sleeping through the night?" Sierra questioned as she swung open the car door and uncoiled from the driver's side leather seat.

"Like a baby, but it's a double edged sword," Ariel replied exiting the passenger side and bumped the door shut with her butt.

Sierra screwed up her nose, "Huh?"

"It means he'll be fit for duty soon and probably headed back to take on more dangerous missions."

"What are you going to do?"

"Nothing. His ambition was to serve his country and I just received a job offer to relocate to Lexington. I'm talking Calumet Farms."

Sierra halted mid-step toward the entrance and ducked her head around, her lips in a perfect O.

"Yes." Ariel confirmed, "My dream job. Sierra?"

"Huh?" Her friend's mouth gaped open.

"Your mouth resembles a fly trap, so close it," she quipped.

Sierra snapped her mouth shut and opened it,

allowing three words to fall out, "Wow, just wow."

"I haven't accepted yet or given notice to Jeff."

"Have you told Gavin?"

"No, because I haven't decided to accept. I'm in love with him, Sierra. In spite of every reason not to be, I am."

Sierra stepped forward and wrapped Ariel in her arms. "You want my advice?"

"Yes, I'm always open to your new age wisdom," she said, resting her head on Sierra's shoulder.

"Get a good night's sleep and we'll toss around all the various scenarios tomorrow," she said, steering the visibly exhausted doctor into the house and into the bed in her guest room. She turned down the covers and stepped aside as Ariel collapsed face first onto the pillow.

Chapter 21

"How'd you sleep?" Sierra asked as she handed a cup of coffee to Ariel.

"Like the walking dead," Ariel answered, a satisfied glow on her face. She savored a long sip from the oversized cup. "Ummm, great espresso, *amiga*."

"My pleasure. Hey, your phone beeped first thing this morning. I didn't want to disturb you." Sierra placed the cell phone on the table in front of her friend.

Ariel gazed at the missed call log. "Oh, it's someone from the university." She tapped the icon for voice mail and listened to the message.

"I take it the surgery was a success?" Sierra asked, observing the elation on the vet's face.

"Indeed." The fact her patient's surgery had gone well and she'd no doubt recover one hundred percent put Ariel one step closer to sitting for her boards and fast tracking to her dream job in Lexington. Being board certified in repro gave her a credential necessary for playing in the big leagues.

"We need to talk, Sierra."

"Does this have anything to do with the conversation we started last night?"

"Yes, and I've made my decision."

"You sound very resolute but I have to ask, are you sure about this? What about your brother and Hottie Mac SEAL? I know you, Ariel and impulsive is not a word I'd use to describe you but this decision seems, well, fast."

"Listen, I know you want what's best for me…"

"Absolutely." Sierra cut her off.

"I realize this is a big change but rest assured I have worked the decision through. Let me fill in some blanks. My offer letter made the assumption I'd sit for and pass the scheduled boards before packing up and moving to Kentucky. The exams aren't for two months so I have a reprieve. I can transfer John from the Naval Hospital to the farm, oversee his recovery in the real world and assess needed modifications for life in a wheel chair before we leave. I also plan to help Jeff in his search for a replacement farm vet."

"Wait a minute. 'We?' You're relocating John to Kentucky?"

Ariel's brow creased in a stubborn line. "I'm not leaving him."

Sierra put her hands up in surrender. "Okay, okay. Have you told him yet?"

Ariel's stomach knotted. She forced the saliva down over the lump in her throat. "No, but I will. I'm committed to ensuring a smooth transition for everyone."

Sierra's eyes softened, "You have me convinced but selling this to Gavin presents a challenge."

Ariel sat silently, mulling over Sierra's words. She rationalized Gavin resuming his duties as a SEAL was for the best. But best for whom? For starters, him. Followed by the other SEALs in his platoon, the Naval Special Warfare Group, make that the entire Navy, oh and the United States of frickin' America.

Sierra leaned close and laid a hand over Ariel's,

her expression earnest. "You said you love him."

"I do but even if Gavin finagled finishing his enlistment in the states, I'd worry he'd resent me for holding him back. Operating on a SEAL team isn't only a job, but a brotherhood, sworn to train together, fight together, and die together." Her chest constricted until she panted for air as the force of her decision hit home. God, this was going to hurt. But it would be temporary, unlike the permanent ache if he returned home in a casket. "I can't be the girl who lives, suffering as a widow for the rest of my life." *Like my mother*.

Sierra relented. Ariel's tunnel vision was obvious. "I'm behind you, my wonderful friend and I'll be here for you, and anything you need."

Ariel nodded. She sucked in a deep breath and flipped open her calendar. "Yikes!" She checked her watch. "I'm supposed to be at the Naval Hospital in two hours and I haven't left Gainesville yet. Can you zip me over to my truck? I still need to pick up the new van the Casualty Assistance Officer left for me at the farm before I can fetch my baby brother."

"Sure," Sierra said as she grabbed her car keys. "Do *moi* a favor and text me when you've arrived safely at Wildwood, will you?"

Ariel waved her hand in the air and gave Sierra an affronted stare. "Jesus, it's broad daylight. I'm not in any danger. Besides, I can take care of myself."

"No doubt about it, but just a quick text for me, please?" Sierra pleaded.

Ariel gave her friend a thumbs up as they jumped in the car and sped toward the university parking lot but a familiar and uncomfortable tickle niggled at the back of her neck and continued its forewarning all the way home.

****

Ariel inhaled the sweet scent of the honeysuckle, which wove a complex pattern in and out of the chain link fence surrounding the Naval Hospital campus, as she wheeled her Marine sibling down the exit ramp of the hospital. The timing of John's relocation to Wildwood Farms was fortuitous. With his move into her cottage, the privacy she'd enjoyed previously would be limited and so would Gavin's ability to indulge in naked sleepovers. John's presence would deflect Gavin's advances and allow Ariel to put distance between them. "Say goodbye to all this luxury you've grown accustomed to, little brother," she said with a snort, rubbing his shoulder. "It's farm work from here on out. No more slacking for you."

"Yeah, right sis," he said, directing his eyes to the motionless limbs situated in the motorized chair.

"Listen John, you can perform plenty of chores at the farm including assisting me with care of the horses and working outdoors. Sure beats the four dirty white walls you've been staring at. We need to keep up with your water therapy too. You'll love the pool." She kept the tone of her voice upbeat so the crack in her heart wouldn't show as she lowered the ramp in the new van the Navy provided her for her brother's transport.

"Nice wheels, sis." He smirked. "Bet you can't do a wheelie out of the parking lot."

"I bet you're right." She laughed, relieved his sense of humor had returned as she backed out of the parking lot. "This pile of metal will take us to Kentucky though."

"Are you kidding me? You got the job?" he asked

obviously excited by the news.

"Well, contingent on passing my boards, but yeah. We could be mowing blue grass at Calumet Farms in a couple of months."

He fiddled with his hands. "I've made so many friends at the Naval complex." His voice drifted off.

Noting his drop in enthusiasm as the reality of the impending repositioning sank in, Ariel sought to reassure him. "You can invite your friends to visit us and we can come back as often as you want."

"I don't know if Dr. Remington mentioned this to you but he offered to take me in as his roommate. We've become good friends, in addition to doctor-patient, and the last thing I want to do is slow you down being a bur…"

She cut him off, "Don't ever say that word. You are not and will never be a burden, e-v-e-r. We can discuss Dr. Remington's offer to let you stay here and live with him but ultimately I want us together. You're my only family and I love you, little brother."

Silence prevailed for the rest of the trip to Ocala as Ariel mulled over her future options. She failed to notice the black truck following two cars behind traveling south on Highway 301.

Chapter 22

Gavin's meeting with the SOCOM Senior Chief at MacDill transpired with the friendliness of a family reunion. They'd served together on a Mediterranean cruise years ago and did more than one hairy mission off the amphibious ship, USS Nassau, in the Middle East.

The Senior Chief was obviously on board with his return to duty as evidenced by his impatience to the staffer on the phone, while securing the necessary preparations for Gavin to hop a C-141 military transport back to the sandy, mountainous hell of Afghanistan. Gavin's excitement level ratcheted up a few notches at the memory of hunting Taliban and dodging bullets but his attention kept returning to a mental image of one chocolate-eyed beauty licking whipped cream off his top lip. He had no doubt he'd be back in her bed as soon as his deployment ended, but she'd need convincing. Lifetime membership in the insular brotherhood didn't mean he had to stay in the Navy and operate in grisly circumstances. His experience made him eligible for a number of coveted contractor positions at SOCOM but could he coax her into waiting for him? Could he persuade her he'd return alive? If cleared for duty he'd have a few days to convince Ariel how much he loved her.

But, first things first. He had to go over the most

recent test results with Dr. Romero and finish this appointment with an 'all clear.' The Senior Chief told him he'd need the medical release to finalize the arrangements. He gazed around the familiar waiting room, scanning the faces of the other waiting patients. Leaning forward, he rested his chin on his fist, tapping his foot impatiently.

"C'mon Doc, I haven't got all day," he mumbled into his fist and willed the door to open.

Dr. Romero's nurse stuck her head through a crack in the door as if responding to the telepathic request, "Petty Officer Mr. Cross?"

Gavin stood and nodded in her direction.

"The doctor's ready for you."

He stuck his hands in his pockets and nervously jiggled his change as he followed her into the exam room.

Dr. Romero's face gave nothing away when Gavin approached him hand extended.

"Hi Doc, have any news for me?"

A good-news grin only another SEAL would understand spread across the doctor's face. "You're cleared for duty, Petty Officer."

Gavin strengthened his handshake and asked, "Did you forward the paperwork to SOCOM yet?" *I hope not because I need to buy myself some time to convince Ariel my freight train of a job won't prevent me from finishing my tour in one piece and coming back to her.*

"No, if you have some unfinished business, I can hold off for a few hours."

Gavin drew his lips into a thin line, grabbing his upper lip with his teeth.

"Or a few days," Dr. Romero countered thrusting

the file against Gavin's chest. "Here's your copy of the test results." He hesitated, a concerned look on his face, "Try not to get killed over there. I couldn't live with the guilt."

"Aye, Aye, Sir," Gavin released a chest deep sigh and retreated out the door.

Under normal circumstances, he'd swagger down the hall, jacked at the idea of rejoining his buddies but damn it all to hell he'd fallen in love. After he swore to himself he'd keep his emotions in check, he'd plunged heart first for a woman who equated military service to a death sentence. She had a valid point of view. Sometimes war resulted in death. He'd been to his share of funerals and comforted screaming, crying children with the idea they might have lost their Dad but they had twenty other willing shoulders to lean on. Then, invariably, some of those surrogates would end up circling the drain in their next deployment. But death didn't scare him. He was used to living beyond the edge. What frightened him the most was losing a soul-deep connection like the one he shared with Ariel. He'd head back to the farm and make his case.

Chapter 23

Winding up the long tree-dotted drive of Wildwood Farms offered Ariel a fresh view of what she would potentially be losing by relocating to Kentucky. The chrome wind spheres atop the breeding barn fluttered in the afternoon breeze with unusual zest. On the trip home she listened to the weather report cautioning travelers of a tropical weather system starting its churn into the Gulf of Mexico and headed toward Louisiana. Storms and hurricanes were part of the package to life in Florida and no one inland in regions like Ocala paid much attention. The dire warnings usually boiled down to a lot of wind, rain, and inconvenience. Storm trackers had refined the art of predicting their path giving local inhabitants plenty of time to hunker down.

"Looks like we're going to get a little weather," Ariel said as she scrutinized the heavy gray clouds blowing in from the coast.

"Oh, Storm Bella is at least twenty-four hours away. The outer bands are teasing us," John added, looking skyward.

"Yeah, you're probably spot-on, as usual." She smiled affectionately at her brother, remembering his uncanny sense of weather prediction even as a six year old.

"We're here," she said, adding a cheerful lilt to her voice as she turned to take in her brother's first reaction to his new home as she put the truck into park in front of her cottage.

"Did you install the ramp?" he asked.

"Not personally but…"

"You know what I mean," he interrupted.

"Jeff had the ramp installed. He wants you to feel at home."

"No, sis. He did it because you're very good at what you do and he wants you to stay. I'm just excess baggage," he said, his tone resigned.

"Not to me, John, or anyone who knows you. I promise you'll like Jeff. He served in the Navy and he understands everything you've been through. He has a son who is a SEAL." Her brother turned his head so fast, she feared he'd suffered whiplash.

"Are you kidding me? The SEAL you've been doing the mattress tango with is your boss's son?" His mood instantly lifted, he feigned a look of horror and broke into fits of bellicose laughter. "Oh sis, you never break the rules, you decimate them," he spurted out between gasps for air.

"I'm glad you're having fun at my expense, dip wad." She pretended indignation and poked him playfully in his arm. "You'll like him too. He can come across as curt and dismissive but he has a wicked sense of humor. He's survived plenty of combat so you two can share war stories."

"I don't want to put a crimp in your love life staying here at the cottage."

"Don't worry. I need a little space right now where he's concerned, you know, to sort through my own emotions which are closing in at one hundred and ten percent." Ariel fought to keep the tear precariously balanced on her bottom eyelid from falling. "It's been hot and heavy and he's getting deployed soon, so a little heartbreak now is worth a complete meltdown later." The roll of moisture drifted down her cheek. She swiped at it. "Let's get you unpacked." She flicked the switch to open the van door and lower the ramp.

"Not until you answer one question," John spoke softly. "Are you in love with him? Is he the one? Cause I've never seen you light up like the Aurora Borealis when you've talked about anyone else."

"Uh, I counted more than one question, short stack."

"Well?"

"Completely and totally, little brother. Which is why I'm seriously considering the job offer to work at Calumet Farms in Kentucky."

"Do you hear yourself, Ariel?" He scowled.

"Perfectly." She punched the button; the van doors slid back and the ramp whirred until it hit the ground. She trotted down the ramp and up the cottage stairs to unlock and open the front door. "I have to run over to the barn. Make yourself at home and decide what you want for dinner. I'll be back in thirty minutes or so. Will you be okay on your own?"

He answered her with his middle finger and a smile.

****

Gavin rolled up behind the new van in front of Ariel's house and adjusted the rim of his new Ray-Ban aviators. With deployment back into the imminent shit storm, he figured he'd get his style on. He spent a bundle on the new shades, which the sales lady assured him only confirmed his movie star good looks. *Ariel must have transferred her brother home. No time like the present to make an introduction. Better get along with him or risk losing her.*

He rapped on the door and stepped back.

The front door opened with a swoosh. Incredulous, Gavin swiped the designer shades off his face and blurted, "Lieutenant? You're Ariel's brother?"

Just as surprised, John returned the question, "Petty Officer Cross, you're my sister's SEAL? I assumed you were still operating in the sandbox?"

"No, I took a detour on a medical leave but I got cleared for duty." The impact of seeing the young Marine rocked Gavin's sturdy emotional shock absorbers. "How's the recovery coming along, lieutenant?"

John locked his hands on the rims of his wheel chair. "The Navy doctors did a great job of putting me back together. Check out my new wheels," he said, his voice matter of fact.

"Sweet." He shuddered at the lame reply but what else could he say? He abruptly changed the subject, "Do you know where your sister is right now?"

"She headed to the barn."

"I want to share some news with her but let's catch up later. I have a few days before I deploy." Gavin started for the door.

"Hey man, I never got a chance to thank you," John called out over the lump in his throat. "If you hadn't taken out the sniper, I'd be dead. We'd all be dead. You saved my life."

Gavin's chest constricted as if someone had punched him with a hammer. He couldn't speak but nodded in understanding. Then ducked out of the house and walked in a restrained, deliberate gait down the path to the barn. His eyes stung and overflowed. He swiped at his cheeks and flipped his sunglasses down to mask the emotion. He wished for a cold beer. The young man was impressive. It must run in the genes. He eyed Ariel approaching all smiles, ponytail swinging back and forth in rhythm with her hips.

"Hey soldier, fancy shades you're sporting." She held up ten fingers. "I give you a ten in the hot dude category."

Gavin grabbed her ponytail and scooped her into a desperate hug, devouring her lips and invading her mouth with his tongue, relishing her taste. She answered his eager advance and snuggled her hips squarely into his crotch, curling her arms tightly around his waist. While her hands slid up and down his back, he dropped soft kisses on her cheeks and the corners of her mouth reluctantly easing off. She moaned when he released his hold. "Hello, Sunshine," he murmured.

"Okay, an eleven," she conceded.

"Are you threatening me?"

"Very funny. More like a promise."

"Well, I already met your brother, so running naked through your house is probably out of the question."

"For now, while he's getting settled."

"He looks good, by the way. Better than I expected after a Humvee landed on top of him."

"Oh, he told you about the accident?"

"He didn't have to. I was there."

"What do you mean, you were there? You two know each other?"

"I was point man in the Humvee with him when

the IED exploded. It blew me off the vehicle and onto the dirt road. John wasn't as lucky."

Ariel stuck her finger in his face and raised her voice in a rant, "You didn't think it was important to tell me you served with my brother and were the SEAL responsible for his security?"

"I didn't know he was your brother." Gavin knocked her finger away as anger swamped him. *How dare she presume to know what happened on the battlefield?*

Ariel fumed and pointed to herself saying aloud, "Armstrong" and then pointed to the cottage where John had rolled onto the porch and was watching the altercation, "Armstrong."

Struggling to stay in control, Gavin yelled, "There are lots of Armstrongs. It's a common name and until recently I didn't know you even had a brother." As a last defense he blurted, "You don't even look alike."

Ariel leaned in, her voice dripping with resentment, and volleyed, "Well, you know now. Take a good look." She angled her head in John's direction. "The kid had a brilliant future lined up until he counted on you for protection, Mr. Navy SEAL." She edged closer. "We're done!"

"What?" Gavin asked, his disbelief palatable.

She repeated in staccato, spitting out each letter, "*We are done. This relationship is over, Gavin.*"

Not willing to accept her ultimatum, he grasped her hand, "Ariel, let me explain."

"I've got all the explanation I need sitting in a wheel chair over there." She pointed in John's direction ripping her hand from his grip.

"Hey sis, what's going on?" John called out as he

started to wheel down the ramp.

Gavin started toward John. "Just a misunderstanding, leiutenant."

"Don't," Ariel warned. "You've done enough. Please leave."

"Not until you hear what I have to say and we sort this out," he insisted.

She brushed past him, her arms flailing over her head in outrage, "Then, I'll leave. I got a job offer in Lexington and I'm taking it." Storming the steps two at a time she blew through the front door and slammed it shut.

Stunned, Gavin lifted his arms in question to John, "What the fuck?"

"Let her cool off. I'll talk to Ariel and find out what's got her so riled."

"She blames me for the Humvee accident and she's right. I should have seen the IED sooner. It was my job to secure the route."

"We were in the middle of a gunfight when the IED exploded. Listen man, I'll deal with my sister. Go do what you need to do."

Gavin, reluctant, nodded his head. He shook hands with John and turned on his heel to unload more bad news, this time to his father. In a matter of days, he was headed back to where he belonged.

Chapter 24

"Hi Remington, you got a minute," Ariel asked, smiling at her brother's doctor and her new confidant. His fresh white smock added to his dashing good looks against the dull backdrop of the Navy hospital's white walls and nondescript equipment lining the hallway.

"Sure Ariel. I have a few minutes before I start my rounds. What's up?"

"I've decided to accept the offer to work at Calumet Farms, so I and possibly my brother will be relocating to Kentucky." She kept her sunglasses on so he wouldn't notice the dark, puffy circles under her eyes, the toll of little sleep.

"Good for you, I think," he answered. "This had to be a hard decision. You said, possibly your brother. How does John feel about living in Kentucky?"

"He doesn't really want to go, you know with his attachments here. I'm reviewing all our options so I was wondering if your offer of room and board still stands. In case I can't convince him to go with me," she added, smiling slightly.

"Of course. What kind of timetable are we talking about?"

"Well, I feel obligated to help Jeff find another vet. He's been more than generous with John and me. But the sooner I can straighten things out, the better."

"Uh, oh. What happened to the budding romance?

If you don't mind me asking?"

"Deception. Heartbreak." If misery had a look she was sure she wore it.

"God Ariel," he folded her in his arms and circled her back with his palms. "I'm sorry. You don't deserve grief like this."

"It's not the first time my heart's been broken but it will be the last," she murmured as she rested her head on the comfort of his broad chest. Surprised by the loud clamor of heavy footsteps coming down the hall, she peered over Remington's shoulder and shimmied back from the embrace as Gavin stampeded toward them, a piece of paper clutched in his hand. His jaw was locked in a stubborn angle and his pale blue eyes were now dark with anger. He halted a few inches from where she stood, dismissing the other man, and spat, "You didn't waste any time getting over me."

She got Gavin's drift and placed her hand on his arm in a reassuring gesture.

He stilled.

She started to explain, "This isn't what you think. Dr. Lewis and I…"

Jerking his arm from her touch, he exploded, "Who you cozy up with doesn't matter to me anymore Ariel. I got my orders." He shook the sheet of paper in front of her face. "I'll be out of your hair and your life in a few short hours. You're free to do whatever or see whoever you want." He nodded belligerently toward the other male. "I'm hopping a transport out of MacDill tomorrow. I'm headed there now."

The SEAL stuffed the folded document in his back pocket and without waiting for a response, squared his shoulders and disappeared down the hall and out of her life.

"He seemed...definite about things." Remington put his hand on her shoulder, concern in his eyes. "But wrong."

"He's definite all right. I'll probably never see him again." She cringed at the finality of him rejoining the fight half way around the world.

"I could try to catch up with Gavin and set him straight?" he offered with a glance down the empty hall.

"No, I screwed things up. Besides, I don't think he's in a listening mood." Her voice wavered and cracked as she continued, "As much as this hurts, maybe it's for the best." She resigned herself to the outcome of a life without Gavin. The man she tried so hard not to love.

Chapter 25

"Ariel, I'm glad you're back. We need to get these horses secured before the storm hits." Jeff pointed toward the ominous clouds racing across the skyline and pretended he was in the dark about what had transpired between his son and Ariel. "The storm is now officially a hurricane. Weather channel has warned residents to take shelter."

She raised her voice in a screech to overcome the wind's rising volume, "I know. The local weatherman reported the hurricane turned toward the coastline instead of maintaining the normal course up the Gulf to Louisiana. Let me get John's help and I'll meet you in the barn."

"Okay, I'm going to check the front gate. Make sure the horses can't get on the road if the paddock fence gets blown down. See you later." Jeff lowered his head and held on to the bill of his cap as he walked like a man on a mission toward the barn.

Ariel scrambled to her cottage, yelling for her brother. "John, hurricane changed course. Scuttle your butt and give me a hand."

"Sure, what do you need me to do?"

"Go in the barn and lock down anything loose. Check to make sure all the halters are on the hooks next to the stalls. I'm going to unlock the paddock gate so we can transfer the horses outside. The lean-to is the only shelter out there so I'll toss a few sandbags on top to reinforce the structure and ensure the roof holds up in the gale force winds."

"Will do, but I want you to know I don't blame Gavin for my accident. We were in the middle of a gunfight. Sniper fire added to the confusion and…"

Ariel placed her index finger on her brother's lips, "Too late, little brother."

He brushed it away. "It's never too late, sis. You need to understand he did his job. There was a target painted on his chest the entire time he rode on the hood of the Humvee."

"I get it John, I do, but right now we have to secure those horses before they react to the wind picking up. I'm surprised they aren't kicking the stall doors down already." She pointed toward the barn. "Daylight's burning."

Her heart ached as John wheeled into the barn, his arms competently circling the large rubber-topped tires on either side of his chair. With everything he'd been through, it'd be easy to wear a chip on the shoulder, but bitterness wasn't part of John's DNA, she mused, as she leaned into the intensifying gusts and hurried past the barn toward the closest paddock. Absorbed in executing the protection protocol for the million dollar horses, she failed to notice the barn door shut and a padlock popped on the crossbar. Ariel fought to overcome the counter force of the wind as she zip-tied the metal cover of the shelter to the wood foundation before she headed back to help John halter the horses.

The pungent smell of gasoline wafted up her nose and into her lungs. She coughed reflexively while following the sharp scent to dark wet spots around the far edge of the barn where thick gray smoke, caught in the currents of the air stream, snaked up along the exterior. She hurried to the entrance and noticed the cross bar down and the padlock hooked in the opening. Alarmed, she rounded the opposite corner of the barn where she spotted flames licking the sides, enabled by the strong gusts of wind.

"Oh God, no," she moaned and raced back to the front of the barn. She pounded on the door with both fists, "John, are you in there?"

"Yeah. The barn's filling up with smoke. It's hard to breath. Hurry sis. Get me out of here."

Her pulse hammered and blood pounded in her ears as she yanked on the unmovable padlock. The frantic bumping of impatient horses stamping against wooden stalls raised the hair on her arms, "I have to get bolt cutters. Roll off your wheel chair. Get down on the floor. I'll be right back." Her orders were answered by a sharp thud.

She whirled around to see Jeff barreling toward her. "Thank God." Not waiting for him to get any closer, she shouted, "Someone locked the barn door with John and the horses inside. We need bolt cutters."

Without hesitation Jeff veered off in the direction of his house and attached garage. "Hose is on the side, next to the driveway." He called over his shoulder. "Wet the roof. I'll call the fire department."

"It's miles away," she called out, but he was already out of hearing distance.

She dashed around the corner and located the hose already hooked up with a spray nozzle attached. Preoccupied with her brother's rescue she bent to turn on the faucet. Her head snapped back. Pain radiated through her skull as someone yanked her hair from behind. She wobbled forward in an attempt to keep her balance.

"Come here, bitch." The voice seethed in her ear.

"Drake, let me go." She screamed, twisting and flailing her arms. "John's trapped in the…You bastard. You did it. You set the fire."

"Bingo, sweetheart." He hissed as he wrapped her ponytail more firmly around his fist and locked her right arm behind her back. "You don't need any distractions from being with me. And you *do* belong to me."

Ariel struggled to right herself as Drake continued to tug her backwards in step with his retreat. A hundred thoughts raced through her mind as the smoke surrounding the barn, filtered into the woods. Fueled by the thought of her brother choking and gasping for air, she pleaded with Drake to release her. "My brother, for God's sake, he needs my help." An eerie blue haze crept along the dense forest floor highlighting the increasing distance between her and John's rescue.

"You won't get away with this." She whimpered, as a briar lanced her arm.

"Oh, and who is going to stop me? Your piece of shit boyfriend you've been shacking up with? I already checked. He's nowhere to be found, darling." He snorted a bone-chilling laugh.

The reality of Drake's statement registered and a stab of fear radiated in Ariel's chest. Saving John and the horses was solely up to her. She clawed at the hand, which gripped her hair and scratched as far down Drake's arm as she could, sinking her fingernails deep into his skin. He yelped and briefly released her, shaking his wounded arm and flinging blood in every direction. She spun around, faced him and forced her knee in his groin sending him spiraling to the ground in agony.

"You fucking witch. You'll pay for what you did to me." His face contorted in rage as he tried to stand.

Ariel backed quickly away from Drake, turned and started running, ducking and dodging low hanging tree limbs and wind tossed branches as she darted for the barn. Twigs snapped behind her and she glanced over her shoulder to find Drake gaining ground. Suddenly air born, she tripped over a log and landed hard on the rain-soaked earth, unable to breathe. The last thing she remembered was the smell of Drake's rank body odor.

Chapter 26

Frustrated, Gavin chucked his useless cell phone in the shotgun seat of his jeep. *Great, no signal.* With his flight out of MacDill cancelled due to the storm, he decided to head back to Ocala and help his father secure the farm. As he sped up the interstate, eerie in the absence of other vehicles, other than the few stragglers still trying to leave, the wind bordered on too high to drive and the first drops of rain pelted his jeep. His stomach rolled and his neck muscles tightened, he could barely turn his head. Dread at seeing Ariel after their explosive split combined with anger at her unwillingness to hear his side, had him second guessing his decision to drive back to Wildwood. He determined the best approach was silence. Not the silent treatment. Just silence and a steely outward composure.

****

A faint vermillion glow on the underside of the clouds distracted him from his churning thoughts as his jeep rolled up to the farm's closed front gate. He stared through the windshield at the glimmer of orange growing in the distance. His stomach plummeted. *Fire?* His senses flipped on high alert and adrenaline surged like a shot to the heart. The worst possible scenario slapped his mind as he pictured his family home in flames. Compelled by necessity, he forced the driver's door of the wind-buffeted car open and unlocked the gate. The wind caught the heavy metal, blowing a gap wide enough for the jeep. Gavin, already back inside, jammed the shift in gear and shot through the opening, not risking the time to secure the latch or padlock. With icy resolve he slammed the gas pedal to the floor and steered the wheels in the opposite direction of the fishtailing tires. The wind howled with the intensity of a freight train as he approached the main property and took his first glimpse of the red and yellow flames intertwined with columns of black smoke billowing into the sky. *The barn. Not the house.*

He sped closer to the spiraling inferno anxious for a view of the paddock where the horses should be housed. *Empty. Where are the horses?* He slammed to a stop and leapt out. The headlights served as a beacon, outlining the thirty-stall enclosure engulfed in flames with no one in sight. A chill ran up his spine as the snorting and stamping of horses emanated from inside the padlocked barn. *Holy shit, the horses are inside. Why is the barn door padlocked? I need bolt cutters, pronto.* Adrenaline spiked in Gavin's system. He plunged forward in a run, but halted dead still when he detected a faint cry carried by the wind.

"Help. Please. Help meeeee."

"*Is the wind playing tricks on me or did I just hear Ariel?*"

Frozen and with his eyes closed, he listened intently, zeroing in on the direction of the noise. The plea for help came from the woods on the other side of the parking lot.

"Please Drake. Let me go. My brother…the horses. I'll go with you. Just open the barn door."

The desperation in Ariel's voice was unmistakable.

In a split second he made his decision. He shoved the grisly circumstances in the barn aside and raced to rescue the only woman he'd ever loved.

The distance between him and his intended target evaporated as Gavin poured on the speed for which he was famous. The outline of trees zipped by as he zig-zagged closer to Ariel's continued pleas for help. When the woods suddenly ended, Gavin had a clear view of Drake dragging and tugging Ariel by her hair twisted in his grip. With Drake almost to his car, Gavin's urgency surged in a final adrenaline burst.

He slammed into Drake at a dead run, plowing into him shoulder first, and knocked him to the ground. Porter sprawled, face down in the dirt, releasing his grip on Ariel.

"Don't get up," Gavin ordered, "you useless piece of shit."

He back stepped over to Ariel and checked her for injuries keeping a watchful eye on Drake. "You okay?"

"Yes, but John. He's in the barn." She choked back sobs as she bent, running her hands through her hair, and then placing them on her knees.

Drake sputtered as he struggled to stand, "Dude, you're going to regret interfering in our relationship."

In one fluid motion Gavin buried his fist in Drake's solar plexus. The man gasped in an audible whoosh before he crumpled into a fetal position, where he lay motionless and silent

"I'm an expert at conflict resolution, *dude*." Gavin glared and with a dismissive shrug turned back to Ariel, "He's not going anywhere. We need to hurry. Can you run?"

"Not as fast as you. *Go*. I'm right behind you," she

stood up and swayed, motioning him to leave.

Gavin charged forward, his calf muscles strained with effort as he leapt across the soaked earth.

Gasping for air he hoped it wasn't too late. The torrential rain now falling would help put out the fire but would magnify the density of the deadly smoke trapping John and the horses.

With seconds to spare, he arrived to find his father cutting through the heavy padlock on the door. "Dad, John's in there."

"I know. The fire department is on its way."

"We can't wait. The barn's going to collapse," Gavin said as he slid the broken padlock off the hasp. "Stand back. It sounds like John got the stall doors unlatched. The horses will stampede out as soon as I call for Nike. They'll all follow her."

He released a piercing whistle as he and his father flung open the barn doors.

A shrill whinny emanated from within the smoky recesses of the barn. In seconds a blur of hooves and manes streamed out the door and fled for the safety of the open paddock.

Ariel limped up, panting, "Where's my brother?"

"He's still inside," Jeff said.

"Not for long," Gavin stated, as he disappeared into the barn, dodging chunks of burning straw. He stooped to determine how much clearance he had from the choking smoke. *About three feet. Enough for Ariel's brother to still be alive.* "John." He waited a few seconds and called out again. "John, can you hear me?" A long, low moan filled the silence. Gavin scuttled forward in a crouched position, his ears tuned toward the sound. The overturned wheel chair rested in front of him with drag marks leading toward a stall. He darted into the stall and located John, barely breathing but alive.

"I'm going to get you out of here, brother." Gavin stooped, cradled John in his arms, keeping low and avoiding the smoke. Showers of embers swirled and dropped to the floor all around them as he progressed toward the open barn doors. His eyes stung, his throat burned, and his back muscles shrieked with the weight of a full-grown man in his arms but the discomfort was minor compared to his need to save John. As he stumbled through the opening, sirens wailed their approach in the driveway. Ariel and his father rushed to aid the two soot-covered men and helped transfer John to a blanket placed a safe distance from the charred beams.

Firemen poured out of the truck unraveling hoses. An EMT rushed to John's side with a portable oxygen kit. Another moved toward Gavin with a similar set up.

"Sir," he shouted over the howl of the tempest, "come with me. I want to check you over."

"I'm okay," Gavin answered in a raspy voice. He swallowed over what felt like sandpaper coating his tongue and throat. "Some water would be good."

The man handed him a plastic bottle and grabbed his elbow, leading him to the rear of the truck.

"Have a seat on the bumper. I want to check you over."

Gavin sat and emptied the water bottle with a deep, long swig, "Ahhhhhh."

"Let's get some oxygen in those lungs while I do a routine exam," he said as he prepared the kit.

Gavin's protest was cut short by a chest deep

cough. He nodded his consent.

The EMT placed a mask on Gavin's face and started the flow of pure oxygen. He lifted a flashlight from a pouch attached to his belt and shined a beam across each tearing eye. A pulse and blood pressure check followed. Gavin accepted the treatment but his attention was on the activities surrounding John and his sister. After five minutes of breathing oxygen he signaled the EMT to remove the mask. "I need to find the guy I hauled out of the fire and make sure he's okay."

The EMT helped Gavin stand and walked him to the cottage where a crowd had gathered inside circling around John.

Ariel had her brother propped against her chest on the sofa. His eyes were closed and oxygen was being administered. His skin, devoid of any color, appeared pasty white.

Gavin's father hugged him, "Very brave but stupid thing you did, son."

"More stupid than brave, I think."

"You saved his life." Jeff struggled with the words as he continued the embrace.

"How's Ariel?" Gavin asked in a low voice.

"She's holding up remarkably well but I know she'd like to talk to you."

"I don't think so," he averted his gaze in her direction and rolled his eyes.

"Son, the only way out of a situation is straight through it." Jeff nudged him toward Ariel.

Their eyes met and Gavin's nerves frayed as he waited for her to vanquish him from her sight.

She mouthed, 'thank you' and then smiled.

He nodded in acceptance.

Her face turned sour as she gasped, "Where's Drake?"

"Damn. Hopefully still out. I'll go check."

"Wait, I hear a siren," she said, tilting her head toward the open door.

"Good ears. Probably the sheriff. I'll go greet him and show him where we left the sack of shit." He stepped off the porch into rain blowing sideways.

A Sheriff's patrol car crested the final hill and skidded to a stop by the fire truck. Gavin jogged over to meet the deputy as he climbed from his vehicle and surveyed the chaotic scene.

"Deputy, come with me. The weasel responsible for all the destruction is detained. Not sure for how long, though."

The officer raised the collar of his raincoat and fell into step beside Gavin as they tramped through the soggy mud. "What the hell happened?"

"For starters, arson, kidnapping, attempted murder," Gavin said, weaving his way through the blowing tree branches and fallen debris.

The sheriff did a double take and drew his gun, pointing it forward and down in expectation.

"I'll fill you in with all the details," he explained, "but he's already in your system for violating a restraining order."

They found Drake, covered in mud, crawling to his car. The officer holstered his gun and lifted his handcuffs off his belt. "You're not going anywhere." The officer confronted Drake as he hauled him up and held him at arm's distance like a feral cat. "Sir, you got any ID?"

Drake sneered at Gavin, and with the flip of a switch, smiled amicably at the sheriff as he handed over his diver's license. "Officer, there's been some kind of mistake. I was here checking on my girlfriend. You know, making sure she was okay with the hurricane and all."

"Mr. Porter, come with me," the sheriff commanded indicating with a wave of his hand he wanted Drake in front. They all walked back to his cruiser in silence. The deputy opened the back door, " Sir," nodding to Drake, "why don't you wait here." Gavin moved to stand in close proximity of the open door and Drake's only escape route while the deputy propped the driver's door half-opened, and climbed into the front seat. Silent, his eyes stayed focused on the blue glow of his cruiser's computer while he studied the screen. After a few minutes he stepped out of the cruiser, and stood beside Gavin. "Drake Porter, you're under arrest for violation of a restraining order...for starters." He proceeded to read Drake his rights and secured him in the backseat.

"Do me a favor and get him the hell off my property. The people here have had enough of this douche bag," Gavin hissed.

"No problem. The only thing you'll see is my tail lights as I head for the county jail." The deputy rolled down his window, "Might need you to come down to the station and give a statement in the next few days."

"No problem." Gavin stuck his hands in his pockets as the cruiser disappeared down the driveway. He wandered back toward the barn accompanied by the faint jangle of coins clinking as he fingered them in nervous anticipation of facing Ariel. Icy resolve would be his best defense. There was no sense in trying to talk it through. There'd been enough hurt handed out. On both sides.

Chapter 27

John stirred and lifted his arm, touching the mask, which covered his face. Ariel sighed a gut deep relief. Her brother was awake and alive. Thank God. She raised him to a sitting position and slid out from under his flaccid body, allowing the EMTs a full examination. Once they rechecked his blood pressure, pulse, heart, and lungs, one of them disconnected the oxygen and offered John a bottle of water before packing up his equipment.

He shakily gulped a swallow and struggled to speak. "Sis, are the horses okay? Did they get out?"

"Yes, thanks to your heroic efforts, little brother." She pointed in the direction of the paddock. "All safe and sound."

"Do I have you to thank for saving me?"

"No, it was Gavin. Fortunately for both of us he showed up just in time."

"Both of us?" He lifted a brow on his ashen face. "What do you mean?"

"Yeah, Drake, or as you refer to him, my punk-ass ex-boyfriend, set the fire and locked you in the barn with the horses." She shook her head in disbelief and stared at her lap. "Then he attempted to kidnap me. I hate to think what would have happened if Gavin hadn't showed up when he did."

"Now you know why having Petty Officer Cross

with me in Afghanistan acted as a lucky charm. This is the kind of guy who always has your back. I tried to tell you earlier if he hadn't been point man, I'd be dead right now." His blood shot eyes widened. "His warning saved us from the full impact of the IED. When it exploded, Gavin got tossed in a ditch on the side of the road and knocked senseless. The impact blew my door off, and I was thrown out, right in the path of the Humvee as it rolled. My legs got pinned. I couldn't free them or escape the enemy shooting at us." He gritted his teeth. "Gavin took out the sniper, sis, and did everything possible to protect me and my men. I'm alive because of him."

Ariel didn't know what to say. Didn't know what to do. A cocktail of guilt and regret walloped her. Nausea rolled in her stomach. She needed fresh air but her wobbly knees wouldn't support her. It was the same feeling of dread and loss she'd had the day soldiers appeared at her mother's door. She was three again. Another military man she loved was going to disappear from her life forever. And it was her fault.

As if John could read her thoughts he offered solace, "Ariel, you can change the outcome of this situation unlike what happened to our father. Go talk to him. Tell him how you feel."

"It's too late. He's leaving as soon as the hurricane blows over. Besides, Gavin is the type of guy who, once something is over, it's really over. He's not someone who forgives easily. Nor is he one who vacillates on his decisions."

"Maybe true Ariel, but if anyone can change his mind, you can. I'm confident of your persuasive skills." He stared at her in the silence for a full minute before adding, "At least try. I know you'll regret it if you don't."

Her shoulders sagged. He was right, of course, but the tiredness from the day's events sapped her willingness to do anything but soak in a hot bath and crawl into a dry bed. "I think a good night's sleep is in order for everyone."

****

The next morning when she woke, her muscles hurt like the devil. She shuffled out of bed. *One leg at a time over the bed's edge.* With both feet on the floor Ariel massaged her sore scalp. Yesterday's nightmare was over. Thanks to a certain Navy SEAL. What to do about Gavin? John's words circled around in her mind, over and over. The man saved her brother's life and hers. She owed him an apology. In spite of everything, when it counted most, he acted.

Resolved to search him out and apologize for her irrational, belligerent behavior, Ariel hastily threw on jeans, a t-shirt, and tennis shoes. She grabbed her brush and swept her long hair up into a ponytail. Peering out of her second story bedroom window, she viewed the devastation from the fire and the hurricane's subsequent wind and rain. What a total mess. At least the storm had rolled across the state very quickly and out to sea leaving only gray-coated skies.

Grateful no loss of life resulted from the chaos, she never the less, ached for Jeff and all the trouble Drake caused. She wound her way down the stairs and out the door, single-minded about her mission. Time to suck up her guilt and face her demons. Except Gavin's jeep wasn't parked in its usual place. She twirled around in a full circle but the jeep was missing. What the hell?

It hit her like a hot rock exploding in her stomach. Grief swelled in her throat. Her chest constricted. He's already gone. No doubt, he couldn't wait to get away from her. Devastated, she choked back sobs as she hung a left and turned down the road to the back pasture. She stumbled forward, dodging fallen tree limbs until she entered a debris free section of road. Sucking in a deep breath, she broke into a run. Her legs lifted and dropped in a steady rhythm while her arms pumped like pistons back and forth. Exercise would help clear her mind, relieve the stiffness, and steady her emotions. The rhythmic tap, tap of the dog tags against her chest as she ran offered her strange comfort, like a piece of clothing she never removed. She lightly touched them and ran her fingers up and down the metal chain before surging ahead in a final sprint to her favorite spot on the farm.

The oak tree stood silhouetted against the murky sky, untouched by the storm. A sense of relief shimmed through her body. The memories of a steamy SEAL encounter flooded back and a warm tingle replaced the relief. God, she blew it, big time. What happened to, 'get the facts, then act,' which is how she operated in her vet practice. But obviously, not in her personal life. She hadn't given Gavin a chance to explain. Instead, she shut him down at the first mention he was with John when the accident occurred. Haunted by her mother's ghost, she failed in her most important diagnosis, her own feelings. Aware her breathing had become labored she slowed to a walk as she neared the tree. Lifting her forearm she wiped the sweat off her face before lowering herself against the broad trunk.

A male voice, curt but familiar, invaded the quiet,

"Even a hurricane couldn't best this ole man."

Her pulse raced as she raised her head and screeched, "Gavin."

His eyes dull and unreadable, he answered in a raspy tone, "Yes."

She continued, "I assumed you'd already left for MacDill. I looked for you this morning but your jeep was gone."

He towered over her, his body erect and his legs apart; he stood sturdy. As she struggled to stand, she gripped his offered hand. A forceful yank landed her flat against his ripped chest. She gasped at the sudden intimacy. "I need to talk to you," she said in a breathy voice. "I owe you an apology. John explained everything. I was wrong. So, so wrong."

Gavin stepped back dropping her hand. "I don't need an apology Ariel, but thanks. In a couple of hours I'll be out of your life and you can resume your so called friendship with the Navy doctor."

Dumbfounded, she took a minute to realize he was talking about Remington Lewis. "Wait, what? You think I, we, no. Dr. Lewis is John's doctor and I'm very grateful to him but not in a relationship way."

"I happened to see the two of you at the hospital and you seemed pretty chummy," he said with his mouth set in a firm, hard line.

"I'm telling you there is nothing between us other than mutual respect and a common interest in John's recovery and well-being." Anger crept into her voice. Here she was trying to apologize and he's acting all high school jealous. Fine. Nothing to lose at this point. *If I'm going down, I'll go in a fireball of honesty.* "It would be impossible for any romance between

Remington and me because I'm in love with you, Gavin." She placed her hands on her hips and braced herself for the avalanche of verbal rebuke. Time seemed suspended as Gavin scanned her face as if he misread her lips.

"When you were with the doctor at the hospital, your face was so, I don't know, expectant, idolizing? The way you looked at him about buried me," he murmured.

"So you hustled the orders to deploy back to the sand trap?"

"Yes," he said, his tone caustic. "You eviscerated me, Ariel."

"I was wrong to judge you without having all the facts. Fear of ending up broken-hearted like my mother motivated my actions. My calculation, regardless of how lame it sounds, was a relationship with a military man equals a complicated and bad outcome." In a predictable gesture, she grabbed the dog tags hanging around her neck.

Gavin stepped forward and took them from her hand. "When you can forgive yourself, you'll have room for someone else's love. Your father's death wasn't your fault and neither was John's accident."

She stepped into his arms and curled into his hug. "I do love someone else. You, Gavin Cross."

Gavin nuzzled Ariel's hair and crooned, "Umm. Smells like sweet lavender. We have unfinished business with this tree, young lady."

"Good thing trees can't talk." She snuggled closer against his warm body and closed her eyes swamped by undeniable love for this military man.

Chapter 28

Gavin tossed the final canvas kit bag in the back of his jeep. "Dawn thirty and almost ready to go," he said as he observed the sun burning through morning fog. He turned to soak in Ariel's beauty. She appeared stoic but the lack of emotion was a front.

"All set?" She forced a smile as she fiddled with her dog tags.

"Just one more thing." He cupped her chin. "Come for a ride with me to our favorite tree." He shifted his hand to her cheek, brushing it with small strokes of his fingertip.

She closed her eyes and gulped, "Ummm, we don't have time for you know what, do we?" Her face softened into a smile as she closed her hand over his.

"Well, I can dream, but no. C'mon. Hop in." He patted her behind as she walked past him.

"The Navy will court martial you if you miss your flight so keep your hands to yourself, mister," she teased, working to keep the mood light.

They rode silently in the jeep but Gavin's mind whirled with excitement as he steadied himself for the most important op of his life. When they arrived at what had turned into their favorite place on the farm, he got out of the jeep first and scurried around to open Ariel's door.

"Whoa, are we on a date?" she asked.

He smiled his answer and led her straight to the bottom of the hundred-year old oak, falling on one knee.

Surprise evident on Ariel's face, she exclaimed, "Gavin, what the…what are you doing?"

"Asking you to marry me, Doctor Armstrong." His smile reached his eyes as he whipped out an exquisite sapphire and diamond ring on a platinum band and offered her the stunning piece.

Her mouth formed a perfect O. "It's beautiful. When did you have time?"

"It was my mother's, with my father's blessing," he explained.

She picked the family heirloom from his hand and held it to her heart. A tear freely rolled down her cheek. "Yes."

A frown immediately formed between her brows, "You are not a cartoon superhero. The danger is real. What if…Promise me…"

He placed a finger on her frown, "Shhhhh. I know what I do is dangerous. I'm fully cognizant my job isn't some Hollywood version of life, but you're my compass, Ariel. You'll guide me home. Don't worry, Babe, I'm gonna make it back. My capacity will mostly be advisory for the final four months of my tour."

She extended her left hand, wrist slightly bent. He slipped the ring on her finger and kissed her.

Stepping back, she bent her head forward, and unclasped the dog tags she'd worn around her neck almost every day of her adult life. "I know you'll come back to me. I'll be waiting for you." She placed them in his palm and squeezed it shut. "I don't need them anymore."

****

Gavin leaned over his bed, stuffing the final olive drab t-shirt in his backpack with his cell phone pinched between his shoulder and ear, like a kid waiting to tell Santa what he wanted for Christmas. Well, in a way it was Christmas. He was marrying the woman of his dreams and he wanted Tony, his closest friend, to be a part of it.

"First Class Petty Officer Sugar Bomb," Tony answered with his usual savoir-faire. "What trouble do you need me to bail you out of this time, Caveman?"

"No trouble brother, just great news. I'm getting married and I want you to be my best man."

Dead silence. *I know he didn't hang up on me. Did he faint?*

"You still there, T man?" Gavin's face contorted into a frown as he pressed the phone harder to his ear. He could picture his friend shaking the phone as if fixing a malfunction.

Tony's baritone voice squeaked, "I must be dreaming because there's no one more determined to stay single than you, Gavin. I've personally witnessed you earning your nickname on more than one occasion."

"This is for real, Tony."

"Dude, you've got to be shitting me. Someone fell for you?" Tony snickered. "Oh, this is going to be fun. A SEAL wedding. High time we enjoyed some pranks and mischief."

"This is exactly why I almost didn't tell you about her. We both know how the guys can be when one of us ties the knot. You are sworn to secrecy. Promise me."

"Too big an ask G," he quipped.

"Come on, man. Just this once. She's beautiful and smart and she loves me. I've never been happier in my entire life." Gavin shuffled his feet, uncomfortable with the heat of a blush on his face. "Are you in? I want to tell her before I leave for MacDill."

"All in, all the time, brother. And don't worry, I got this locked down."

Chapter 29

Four Months Later

"Looking good, Jeff, "Ariel said, dusting off her hands. "With the renovations complete we're back in business."

"Yeah. Just in time for birthing season." He loaded the last bale of hay in the back of his pickup truck. "Don't you have somewhere to be?"

She grinned and checked her watch. "You want to come?"

"I wouldn't miss it. Besides, I'm your ticket into MacDill. I have a surprise. "

She looked at him expectantly, "What did you do?"

"I called in a favor. I figured you'd like to meet Gavin on the tarmac as soon as he disembarks."

Ariel threw her arms around his neck and hugged him. "You figured right, Boss."

He corrected her, "It's Dad, Ariel. We're family now."

Unable to swallow past the lump in her throat, she pointed toward the house indicating she was going to get ready and walked quickly away.

****

"Ariel, I'm going to park the truck. You go ahead. The special pass you're holding will allow you to enter the restricted area and from there, your military escort will accompany you out on the tarmac."

She leaned over, gave him a peck on the cheek, and jumped out of the truck.

Her escort, waiting inside the terminal, was easy to spot with his MP badge. He smiled and nodded in the direction of the tarmac, indicating she could step through the door.

A plane approached the runway and as the landing gear dropped so did her stomach. Due to Gavin's insane schedule and the nature of his work, their communication had been severely limited. Then there was the eight hour plus time difference. She had a nagging feeling he'd been out on ops even though he assured her he was in no danger. *Huh.* Like she believed pigs could fly. But she understood and accepted he did it to protect her from her past. The plane taxied to a halt. She wiped her wet palms on her slacks and squeezed her arms to her sides absorbing the rolling drops of perspiration. The motorized whir of the C-141's back ramp lowering buzzed in her ears. Her heart raced. She took deep breaths and told herself to stay calm as legs in camouflage pants appeared, descending the ramp.

Among the twenty or so SEALs all joking and talking as they approached the gate, a familiar laugh set her heart on fire. Gavin, unaware she'd be waiting for him, was casually walking, his arm in a sling, sharing a joke with one of his teammates. She couldn't hold back. In a carefree half skip, half run, she cut a beeline straight to him, throwing herself into his embrace. She wrapped her arms around his neck and smooched his cheek.

Surprised, he cut his laughter short, grabbed her in

a one-armed bear hug, and turned his face, capturing her lips in a slow, hard press. The other SEALs immediately hooted and made catcalls in the couple's direction.

"What happened to your arm? Are you okay?" she asked, breaking the hot embrace before the SEALs could form a man circle around them and tease them into tomorrow.

"Oh, it's nothing. Just a strained muscle."

One of the other SEALs in earshot of their conversation joked, "Yeah, he lost at arm wrestling."

Gavin shot him a look that screamed, *SHUT UP*.

Ariel made a mental note to get to the bottom of what really happened to his arm but for now she simply wanted to breathe him in, touch him, and have wild monkey sex.

"Are these the SEALs you deployed with?"

"No, these jokers aren't in my platoon. I caught a hop down here with them from Norfolk."

As if he could read her concern he offered, "I'll live."

She beamed up at him, "Glad to hear it because we have a lot of living to do."

Gavin hugged her closer, tight to his chest. "Together." He kissed the top of her head. "For the rest of our lives." And sighed in her ear, "Forever in Ocala."

A word about the author...

With close ties to the Navy SEAL community, Connie's mission as a writer is to offer the reader a realistic portrayal of men who transfer their alpha tendencies and athletic prowess into serving a noble cause.

A former English teacher and corporate executive, Connie holds a B.S. from East Carolina University. Although she continues her role as Vice President in a busy ad agency, her first love has always been writing. She maintains a portfolio of songs, poems, and stories she wrote as early as ten. When she isn't working or writing, Connie enjoys Zumba fitness and claims her best story ideas come to her while dancing.

Connie lives with her family and two adorable Westies near the Gulf Coast of Florida.

http://www.connieyharris.com